COME TO THE CIRCUS

COME TO THE CIRCUS

ENID BLYTON

Armada

First published in the U.K. by
George Newnes Ltd. First published in this
edition in 1973 by Wm. Collins Sons & Co. Ltd.,
14 St. James's Place, London S.W.1.

This edition 1974

© Enid Blyton 1948

Printed in Great Britain by
Love & Malcomson Ltd.,
Brighton Road, Redhill, Surrey.

A NEW HOME FOR FENELLA

"FENELLA! Where are you?" called Aunt Janet's voice. "Come here a minute. I've got something to tell you."

Fenella put down her sewing and went to see what her aunt wanted. She was ten years old, small for her age, with a little pointed face, green eyes and a shock of wavy red hair. She had no father or mother, and had lived all her life with her Aunt Janet.

Her aunt was peeling potatoes in the kitchen. She looked up as Fenella came in. "Help me with these," she said. "Fenella, I've got some news for you."

"What is it, Aunt Janet?" asked Fenella, suddenly feeling that the news wasn't going to be very good.

"Well, Fenella—I'm going to be married," said Aunt Janet. "And I'm going out to Canada."

"Oh, Aunt Janet!" said Fenella. "To Canada! That's a long way, isn't it—far across the sea? Shall we like that?"

"*I* shall," said Aunt Janet. "I've been there before. But you're not going, Fenella. I'm going to marry Mr. White—you've seen him here sometimes—and he wants us to go and work on his uncle's farm in Canada. But we're afraid we must leave you behind."

"Leave me behind—here, all alone!" cried Fenella in alarm. "But what shall I do? I'm only ten."

5

"Oh, you won't be left here, in this house," said Aunt Janet. "You're going to your Uncle Ursie's. He and Auntie Lou will look after you now. I've told Auntie Lou how good you are at sewing, and she wants somebody she can train to help her with the circus dresses."

"Am I to go and live at the circus?" cried Fenella, and her eyes filled with tears. "I can't. I can't. You know I'm afraid of animals. And there are bears there, and elephants, and chimpanzees. I know, because Uncle Ursie told me so when he came here to tea with Auntie Lou."

"Oh, you'll soon learn to like animals," said Aunt Janet, emptying the dirty potato water out of the bowl. "Anyway, there's no help for it, I'm afraid. You've got to go somewhere—and Harry—that's Mr. White I'm going to marry—he doesn't want to take you out to Canada with us."

"Nobody wants me!" wailed Fenella, suddenly. "My father and mother are dead, and you don't want me, and I know Uncle and Aunt won't want me either."

"Now, don't be silly," said Aunt Janet, briskly. "Uncle Ursie is very, very fond of his bears, and he'll be fond of you, too. As for Auntie Lou, she's got a sharp tongue, but if you are a good girl and help her, she'll soon take to you. I'll miss you, Fenella—you're a good, quiet little thing—but what Harry says has got to be done."

Fenella went back to her sewing. But she couldn't see to stitch any more, because the tears would keep coming into her eyes and dropping on the dress she was making. It wasn't much of a home, with Aunt Janet— just a little cottage, rather tumbledown, with a yard behind it—but at least it was somewhere she knew and felt safe in. And although Aunt Janet made no fuss of her, and sometimes grumbled because she had to bother with her, still, she was kind in her way.

But the circus! That was quite a new world—a frightening world to Fenella, who ran away if she saw

6

even a gentle old sheep, and screamed if a dog jumped up at her. Whatever in the world would she do in a place where elephants and bears, monkeys and dogs roamed about all the time? She couldn't go there. She couldn't.

She thought of Uncle Ursie and Auntie Lou. Auntie Lou had screwed-up hair, a screwed-up face, and a screwed-up mouth. Her tongue was sharp, and she had very little patience with anyone, not even with her slow-going, placid husband, Uncle Ursie, who looked after the bears, and was really rather like a bear himself, clumsy, lazy and a little stupid.

Fenella thought of the three elephants, and the two hairy chimpanzees that Uncle Ursie had told her about. She had never been to his circus, so she could only imagine everything—and it seemed very frightening indeed.

"There'll be monkeys about—and I shall keep meeting the elephants—and, oh dear, Uncle Ursie will expect me to like his awful bears! I don't want to go. Oh, why can't Aunt Janet take me to Canada with her? I don't want to go there either, but I'd rather go across the sea to a faraway land than go and live in the circus. I shall just HATE it. I know I shall."

Poor Fenella! Her whole world seemed to be turning upside down. Aunt Janet began to pack her things. She sold most of the furniture in her little cottage. Strangers always seemed to be coming in and looking round at this and that.

Then the day came for Aunt Janet to be married. She had bought some pretty blue stuff for Fenella to make herself a bridesmaid's dress. Fenella was a marvel with her needle. She could make anything! She knew how to use a sewing-machine, too, and was really a clever little girl. She made her blue dress carefully, but she didn't want to wear it!

"I don't want to see Aunt Janet married. I don't want to say good-bye to her. I don't want to leave here!

7

Oh, why did all this happen?" poor Fenella said over and over again to herself.

But Aunt Janet *was* married, and Fenella did wear her blue frock, which everyone said looked lovely. Then Aunt Janet kissed her good-bye, and drove away with Uncle Harry, waving till she was out of sight.

Uncle Ursie and Auntie Lou hadn't come to the wedding, because the circus was rather far away just then, and was about to put on a show. Janet was to be put on the train, in the care of the guard, and was to go off to the town where the circus was, all by herself. She was full of dread about this.

"But it will be quite an adventure for you, Fenella!" big, burly Uncle Harry had said.

"I don't like adventures," Fenella had answered. And she didn't. She was afraid of them. She didn't like strangers. She didn't like anything she didn't know. She was a scared little mouse, as Aunt Janet had often said.

And now she was to go and live in the middle of a big circus. It was a world of its own, with tall, shouting Mr. Carl Crack, the ringmaster, as its king. Fenella had heard about him from Aunt Janet, and she felt afraid of him already. Mr. Carl Crack! She pictured him with a big whip, cracking it if anyone disobeyed him. Oh dear! She would hide away in a corner if ever she saw him.

Mrs. Toms, her next door neighbour, came up to her, smiling kindly. The wedding was over. The guests had gone. Fenella stared forlornly round.

"Well, Fenella, dear, you come along with me now, as your auntie said, and we'll get you out of that pretty frock and into your brown one. Then off we'll go to the station to catch that train. And in no time at all you'll be off to the circus—my, what a lucky girl you are!"

Fenella didn't say anything. She went home with Mrs. Toms. Mrs. Toms had five children, all rough and loud-voiced. They crowded round Fenella and told her how lucky she was to be going to live in a circus.

"Wish *I* could!" said Sam, the eldest. "My word, I'd ride all the horses, and the elephants, too!"

"And I'd make friends with the chimpanzees and teach them all kinds of things," said Lucy, a big curly-haired girl with a wide smile. "I'd love to have one for a pet. You'll have a lovely time, Fenny."

"I shan't," said Fenella. "I shall hate it. I don't want to go a bit. I wish one of you could go in my place, and I could stay here."

"Oh, you'll soon get used to it, and you'll wonder why you didn't want to go," said Mrs. Toms, briskly. "Now, are you ready? Sam, take Fenny's bag. That's right. Who wants to come and see her off?"

Everyone did, though Fenella would really rather have gone alone with kind Mrs. Toms. Her children were so *very* rough and noisy. The shy little girl hated walking to the station with such a crowd of shouting children round her. But they meant it kindly, and were sorry for her.

"Come along quickly—the train's just coming in!" cried Mrs. Toms. "Here's your ticket, Fenny. Let us on to the platform, please, Inspector, we're just seeing this child off!"

Fenella was pushed into a carriage. Mrs. Toms hurried to ask the guard to keep an eye on her during the journey. The children all crowded round Fenella, and Lucy gave her a hug.

"Write to us! Tell us about the elephants and what their names are!"

"Be sure to tell us if you like the bears your uncle has!"

"Do make friends with the chimpanzees and tell us what they're like!"

"Good-bye, Fenny! Cheer up! Good-bye!"

"Good-bye! You're off!"

The train steamed slowly out of the station. Fenella waved till she could see the Toms family no more. Then she sat back on her seat, feeling sad and forlorn. She had left her only friends behind. Aunt Janet was off to Canada. And here was she, Fenella, going to an uncle and aunt she hardly knew, and who she felt sure didn't really want her—to a place full of roaring, growling, barking animals!

There were two old ladies in the carriage, but they took no notice of the little girl at all. Once or twice the guard came in to see if she was all right. She had a packet of sandwiches with her, and when the guard told her it was one o'clock she ate them. Then she fell asleep, whilst the train rocked over the rails at sixty miles an hour.

When she awoke, the guard was in her carriage again. "Wake up, Missy! You're there! This is Middleham, where you've got to get out."

Half asleep, Fenella got hold of her bag, and scrambled out of the train. She stood on the platform and watched it go off. Then she turned to go out of the station. Aunt Janet had told her what to do next. She had to give up her ticket and then ask where the bus started that went to Upper Middleham, where Mr. Carl Crack's circus was.

A porter told her. "There it is, Missy—over there in the corner of the station yard. Hop in. It will be going in a minute or two."

She got in. "I want to go to Mr. Carl Crack's circus," she told the conductor. He gave her a ticket and took a penny from her. "I'll tell you when to get out," he said.

The bus lumbered through the countryside, and at last climbed a hill, and then slowed down on the slope the other side. "Here you are!" called the conductor. "This is the circus field."

Fenella got out. She stood looking down on the circus field, her heart sinking. There was the circus, the place she was to live in.

Gay caravans stood everywhere, with smoke coming from some of their chimneys. Tents were here and there. Travelling vans were pulled up at one end of the field.

A very, very big tent stood in the middle, a flag waving from the top. Painted on the tent were four enormous words.

"MR. CARL CRACK'S CIRCUS."

Fenella had arrived. Now her new life was to begin!

MR. CARL CRACK'S CIRCUS

FENELLA put her bag down on the ground and climbed a gate nearby. She sat on it and looked at the big circus field. What a lot seemed to be going on!

Men and women walked about busily. Horses were being cantered at one end of the field. Fenella could hear the men shouting to them.

Then she saw an enormous elephant lumbering along, waving his trunk. Beside him walked a very small man indeed. Fenella felt scared. She made up her mind she would keep as far away from the elephants as she possibly could. What big ears they had! And what funny little eyes.

Not far off was a small woman with something round her shoulders. At first Fenella thought it was a fur. Then, to her great astonishment, she saw that it was two tiny monkeys, each clinging tightly to their owner. The little girl shivered. How could anyone have monkeys round their necks?

Then a pack of barking dogs was suddenly set free from a big travelling cage, and to Fenella's horror they came tearing over the field towards her. But they swerved away as they came near and went over to the big elephant. They ran in and out of his legs without fear, and the big creature was very careful where he put his feet down.

As she sat there, a man came over towards her. Fenella looked hard at him, and then saw that he was her uncle. She hardly knew him because he looked very different from when she had seen him last.

He had come to tea with Aunt Janet, his sister, looking very smart and clean and neat in a well-brushed Sunday suit, and a bowler hat.

Now he was dressed in a very old, very dirty pair of flannel trousers, and a brightly striped jersey; his hair was long, and standing up all over the place. He had little eyes, and a big nose and mouth. Fenella couldn't help thinking he looked a bit like a bear, for he was fat and clumsy. But he looked quite kind.

"So you've arrived, Fenella!" he said. "Come along and see your aunt. We've been expecting you for the last half-hour. Had a good journey?"

Fenella nodded. She didn't like the look of Uncle Ursie to-day. He looked so dirty and plump and clumsy. He grinned widely at her and his little eyes almost disappeared. He held out a very dirty hand.

"Come along. Don't be shy. My, what a neat, prim-looking little thing you are! Like your Aunt Lou. Never a thing out of place with her. Too tidy altogether for my liking!"

Uncle Ursie was very talkative. Fenella didn't really need to say a word. He pulled the little girl along over the big field, carrying her heavy bag for her.

They passed a man doing the most extraordinary things. As they came by, he suddenly bent himself right

12

backwards till his head went between his legs and came out at the other side. His face grinned at Fenella from between his knees. She was frightened.

"Don't you worry about old Wriggle," said Uncle Ursie. "He's one of our acrobats. Regular contortionist he is. He can do anything with that rubbery body of his. He'll pull it inside out one of these days."

They came to a neat red caravan with blue wheels. "Here we are!" said Uncle Ursie proudly. "Do you like it? Pretty, isn't it? The blue wheels were your aunt's idea, and the blue chimney, too. Hey, Lou, are you there?"

Aunt Lou appeared at the door of the caravan. It was at the back. Fenella looked up at her. She saw a small neat woman, dressed in a dark blue cotton frock with red spots and a red belt. Her hair was screwed up in a tight bun at the back, and her eyes and mouth looked tight, too. She gave Fenella a thin kind of smile.

"Oh, there you are! I've kept dinner for you. Come on in and eat it."

Fenella went up the steps of the caravan. She looked round. Inside it was a room full of furniture. On one side was a broad seat, that Fenella saw would be a bed at night. On the other side, folded up out of the way, was a narrow bunk. That would be for Fenella.

"Do you live in this caravan?" she asked. "Don't you ever live in a house?"

Aunt Lou gave a snort. "In a house! What do you take us for? I wouldn't live in a house, not if you gave me a hundred pounds! How could you live with a circus if you have a house with roots in the ground! No, no—you want a house on wheels, so that you can go where you like. Now, here's your dinner."

Fenella was just going to say that she had had some sandwiches, when she smelt the good smell of the dinner. She decided to eat it and sat down. It was certainly very good.

"Your aunt's a good cook," said Uncle Ursie, watching

Fenella eat. "And you won't find a cleaner caravan than ours! No, nor a more comfortable one. I'll say that for your Aunt Lou, she's a worker, she is—and a wonder with her needle, too!"

"Stop your talk," said Aunt Lou. "Get along and do some work, Ursie. Leave Fenella to me."

Uncle Ursie clambered down the steps to the ground, and the whole caravan shook as he went.

"Big and clumsy as a bear," said Aunt Lou, in a sharp voice. "Now you eat all that up—and there's some fine peaches in syrup for you, too."

"It's kind of you, Aunt Lou," said Fenella, timidly. She was afraid of her sharp-faced aunt.

"Well, I expect something in return," said Aunt Lou. "You're clever with your needle, aren't you? Well, I shall expect you to help me with the sewing. I've too much for one pair of hands to do."

"What sewing?" asked Fenella.

"I sew for all the circus folk," said Aunt Lou. "There's always plenty of dresses to be made, and you wouldn't believe how careless people are with their things. Mending, mending, mending! You just look at that!"

Fenella looked at the corner where her aunt pointed. Piled there was a heap of gaily-coloured skirts and coats, stockings and jerseys. Fenella leaned forward and picked up a very small coat indeed. She looked at it curiously.

"Whose is this?" she said. "It looks as if it would only fit a doll! I've got a doll called Rosebud. It would just about fit her!"

"Oh, that belongs to one of Mrs. Connie's monkeys," said Aunt Lou, in such a disagreeable voice that Fenella looked at her in surprise. "I don't know why I've got to sew for monkeys, the dirty little creatures! But that Mrs. Connie, she says she doesn't even know how to thread a needle, the lazy creature—so Mr. Crack has told me to dress-make for the monkeys, too. Bah!"

Fenella couldn't help thinking it would be lovely to

14

make little coats and dresses for monkeys, even though she knew she would be afraid to fit one on. She went on with her dinner, enjoying the peaches in their sweet juice.

"Well, I'll help you with the sewing, Aunt Lou," she said. "I'd like to. I love sewing. And I can use a sewing-machine, too."

"Well, that's a thing you'll have to do without," said Aunt Lou. "A sewing-machine, indeed! We're not millionaires. Now, have you finished? Well, you go and tell your uncle I want him to go and buy some sausages, or he won't have any supper to-night."

Fenella didn't at all want to go out alone in the big circus field, with so many strange people ambling about, and animals appearing round any tent. But she didn't like to say so, because Aunt Lou wasn't the sort of person who would like that at all.

So the little girl went timidly down the caravan steps and looked about for her uncle. She saw him not far off and went across the grass to him.

CRACK! A loud noise, like a pistol-shot, made her jump almost out of her skin. Something touched her lightly and she drew back, wondering what it was.

Then a loud voice roared at her. "Get out of the way, ninny! What are you doing over here? Nobody's allowed in my part of the field. Serves you right if you got licked by my whip! "

Fenella turned and saw an enormous man, burly and big-headed, with a grey top-hat on his head, standing not far off with a whip in his hand. He had a big nose, and great brown eyes, topped by the thickest, shaggiest eyebrows that Fenella had ever seen. It was the eyebrows that frightened her most.

The voice went on roaring at her. "Who are you? No one is allowed in this field unless they belong to the circus. Clear out! Mind the dogs don't bite you! Mind the bears don't eat you! I won't have children wandering about my camp! "

Fenella was so very frightened that she ran away at top speed. She didn't stop till she got to the field gate. She climbed over it and ran down the lane, then into another field. She lay down under a gorse bush, panting.

"It must have been the great Mr. Carl Crack himself!" she thought. "Oh, dear. I never saw that he was standing there and cracking his whip. It almost touched me. What a terrifying person he is! I daren't live in his circus. I daren't, I daren't. I shall run away. I shall go to the next town and go and live with a dressmaker there, and earn money by helping her. I'll never, never go and live in Mr. Crack's circus. Why, he looked as if he could eat me!"

Fenella was tired and scared. She began to cry softly. Then she heard a curious sound and sat up. It came from the other side of the thick gorse bush.

It was the sound of birds singing and whistling. It went on and on. Birds flew down from trees to the other side of the bush. The whistling changed to a curious chirrupping, and at once a dozen nearby sparrows chirruped back.

Fenella dried her eyes. She crept softly round the bush, and peeped. She saw a most curious sight.

On the grass, sitting up straight, was a boy of about twelve. It was he who was whistling so like the birds. Round him, some on branches, some on the ground, were all kinds of wild birds, enchanted by his calls.

But, most extraordinary of all, was a big bird squatting beside him. It was a large white goose! Fenella could hardly believe her eyes.

Suddenly the goose saw her and cackled loudly. All the birds flew away. The boy turned and saw her.

"Hallo!" he said. "Who are you? I'm Willie Winkie the Whistler. And this is my pet goose, Cackles. Come and talk to me. Why have you been crying? You come along and tell me, Green-Eyes. We'll soon put things right for you!"

16

THE BOY AND THE GOOSE

FENELLA stared at the boy without saying a word. He had pale gold hair, so fair that it was almost white. His face was completely covered with freckles, and he had a dimple in each cheek that went in and out when he smiled. He was smiling now.

"Come on, silly," he said, and held out his hand. "You're not frightened of old Cackles, are you? She's a darling. Shake hands, Cackles."

To Fenella's great surprise the large goose stood up and, balancing herself awkwardly on one leg, held out the other foot to Fenella. It was a large, webbed foot, and the little girl didn't want to touch it.

"Oh, go on," said the boy. "Don't be mean. Cackles will be awfully hurt if you don't shake hands. I tell you, she's the friendliest goose in the world. Aren't you, Cackles?"

"Cackle," said the goose, agreeing. She still held out her paw, and Fenella at last took it and gave it a feeble shake. It felt cold and clammy. The goose sat down again and put her big, yellow beak on the boy's shoulder.

"Now, you tell me why you've been crying," said Willie. "Anyone been unkind to you?"

"Yes," said Fenella, tears coming to her eyes again. "Mr. Carl Crack has. He shouted at me and told me to clear out, and he was so angry that I ran away. I shall never go back."

"I say! Are you Ursie's niece?" said Willie, sitting up straighter. "I heard you were coming, but I thought you'd be a lot bigger. How old are you?"

"Ten," said Fenella. "I used to live with my Aunt

17

Janet, but she's married and gone to Canada. I haven't got a father or mother. They died when I was little. So I've got to come and live with Uncle Ursie and Aunt Lou. And I don't like them. I don't like anybody I've seen at the circus. And I am so scared of all the animals, too. I'm going to run away! "

"No, you're not," said Willie, and he put an arm round her. "Wipe your eyes, silly. You'll love living with us after a bit. Fancy wanting to live an ordinary life, in a house, when you can live in a circus, with animals all round you, and have a house on wheels that can take you away wherever you like! "

"I'd rather not," said Fenella. "I'd rather run away."

"But you'd only be brought back," said Willie. "You would, really. And then everyone would be very cross with you, which would be a pity. I tell you there are lots of nice people in Mr. Crack's circus. I'm one of them! And my mother is another. I haven't got a father, so I look after my mother and she looks after me! And Cackles looks after us both. Don't you, Cackles?"

"Cackle," said the goose, and made a little hissing noise in Willie's ear.

"Don't," said Willie. "You tickle. Move up a bit, Cackles. You're leaning too hard on me."

Cackles moved up. Fenella watched in surprise. "Does she understand everything you say?" she asked.

"Everything! " said Willie, with a grin. "I had her when she was a gosling—that's a baby goose in case you don't know—and I found her half dead down a lane. Goodness knows how she got there, poor mite. I took her to Mum, and we warmed her and fed her— and here she is, simply enormous, the Cleverest Goose in the World! I take her in the ring with me when we give a show."

"Do you really?" said Fenella, opening her eyes wide in wonder. "But what can she do?"

"Oh, she's a marvel! " said Willie. "She wears a red shawl and a cute little bonnet, and she carries a shopping basket under her wing. And I'm the shopkeeper, and she buys what she wants from me. I tell you, we bring the house down, me and Cackles! "

"I'd like to see you in the circus-ring with Cackles," said Fenella.

"Well, it's no good your running away then, or you won't," said Willie. "You stay with us and you'll soon get to know us and like us."

"But I'm so afraid of Mr. Crack now," said Fenella, remembering that enormous voice of his.

"You don't need to be," said Willie. "He's the kindest fellow really—but he's hot-tempered, and maybe he didn't see you and was afraid he'd hurt you with his whip-cracking—so he roared at you to get out of the way. If he'd known you were Ursie's niece and had come to live at the circus, he'd have been kinder. But a whole lot of town kids are always wandering about the field, scaring the monkeys and sometimes opening cage doors. He gets wild with them."

"Oh," said Fenella. Then she remembered something. "Willie, what were you doing when I heard you whistling? I saw a lot of birds round you."

"Well, I told you I was Willie Winkie the Whistler, didn't I?" said the boy. "Want to see what I can do? All right then—watch."

Fenella sat absolutely still. Cackles took her head from the boy's shoulder and curled it under her wing. She sat still, too. Then Willie began to whistle like a blackbird.

"Phooee, phoo, phee-dee-ee, phoolee dooee," he whistled, sounding like a flute. Fenella gazed at him in amazement. How could he sing like a bird? Nobody would know it wasn't a bird singing! A nearby blackbird answered the whistling boy and flew nearer. Willie fluted back, and the bird drew nearer still. Then the boy changed his song and imitated the chaffinch's merry rattle. One answered him and soon two or three came round.

19

Willie whistled like a great-tit. "Pee-ter-pee-ter-pee-ter, pee!" he whistled. And three great-tits answered and came flying down.

Soon there was a ring of birds round the boy, who, except for his mouth, did not move at all. Fenella kept as still as a mouse, fascinated. The goose did not stir a single feather.

Robins came when Willie imitated their rich, creamy little song. Thrushes came, and a wagtail, too, calling its musical "chissik, chissik," in answer to Willie. Fenella had never seen birds so close in her life. One of them actually hopped on to Willie's foot. Then a robin flew to the top of his head and carolled loudly.

Cackles uncurled her long neck and hissed. The robin flew off in alarm. So did the other birds.

"Oh, Cackles! You shouldn't mind if a robin perches on my head!" said Willie, laughing. He stroked the soft feathers of the goose, who hissed softly and pecked lovingly at his hand.

"She's jealous if any bird comes too near," said Willie. "Well, what did you think of all that?"

Fenella looked at Willie with shining eyes. "I think you're wonderful," she said. "Oh, Willie—how do you do it?"

"Little secret of mine!" said Willie, and he laughed. "Like to see it?"

"Oh, yes!" said Fenella. Willie put his hand into his mouth, and then took out what looked like a cherry-stone with a hole in it. "That's my secret," he said.

"But—what does that do?" asked Fenella, puzzled.

"I fix it in between two of my teeth," said Willie. "And it helps me to make all those whistling noises. My father used to imitate birds, too. He had a lot of these stones and things. I found them and practised with them. It's in our family. My great-uncle was a famous bird-whistler, too."

Fenella couldn't understand how a little cherry-stone with a hole in it could possibly help Willie to make all those bird-noises. He popped the stone back into his mouth, and did a few trills. It was marvellous.

Cackles stood up and began to peck at the grass hungrily. That made Fenella suddenly remember something. "Oh dear! I've just remembered! Aunt Lou told me to tell Uncle Ursie to buy some sausages for his supper to-night—and I forgot."

"Well, we'll go and fetch them," said Willie. "Come on. That will put your aunt in a good temper! Hey, Cackles, coming?"

Cackles came with them. Fenella was afraid that the dogs they met might snap at her, but Cackles was not afraid of any dog in the world. One peck from that big beak and the biggest dog would fly howling down the street!

The three of them, much stared at, arrived in the little town of Upper Middleham. Willie bought some sausages. Then he bought a bar of chocolate for Fenella. She was very pleased.

"You *are* kind!" she said. "I don't think I'm going to run away after all. It won't be so bad if you're there. I'd like to be friends with you and Cackles."

"Cackle," said the goose, and pressed against the little girl.

"There you are!" said Willie. "She says she'll be friends with you, too! We'll have some fun, Fenny. I'll take you round the circus and introduce you to everyone. You needn't be afraid if *I'm* there! Even the elephants eat out of my hand."

Fenella thought that Willie Winkie was the most wonderful boy she had ever met. What twinkling eyes he had! What a lot of freckles—and what funny little dimples! She had never seen a boy with dimples before, but they suited Willie. She wished she had one, too, that went in and out when she smiled, like Willie's. But she hadn't.

They went back to the circus. Fenella felt nervous when they went in at the gate. Suppose she met Mr.

Crack again, with his enormous whip. She would want to run away!

They did meet him. He came swinging round the corner, humming loudly, leading a most beautiful black horse. "Hallo, Willie Winkie!" he said. "How's old Cackles? And who's this young lady with red hair and green eyes?"

Fenella trembled. Surely he would know she was the little girl he had roared at not so long before.

"This is Fenella, Ursie's niece, who's come to live at the circus," said Willie. "She's to help Lou, you know, with the sewing."

"Oh, so you're Fenella!" said Mr. Crack, and he fished in his pocket. He brought out a bag of sticky sweets. "Here you are then, girl. Sweets for you, and don't you give any to that greedy goose. And mind now, if anyone scares you, or shouts at you, you just come to me, Mr. Carl Crack—and I'll crack my whip at them and scare them into fits! Ho ho ho, that's what I'll do!"

He stood towering over Fenella, his face one big kind smile. The little girl couldn't help smiling back as she took the sweets. He didn't seem a bit like the man who had roared at her a few hours back.

Willie took her hand. "What did I tell you?" he said. "You don't need to be scared of Mr. Crack—unless you do wrong. But you're a good little girl, I can see. Come along and meet my mother. We're going to have a fine time together, you and Cackles and I!"

WILLIE took Fenella to his caravan to meet his mother. "This is my Mum," he said. Fenella looked at his mother. She was thin and worn-looking, with untidy brown hair with a good deal of grey in it, and she looked untidy in her dress, too. She needed a button on her blouse, and a hook on her skirt. Both were done up with big safety pins.

But she had dimples just like Willie's, and such a lovely smile that Fenella liked her at once.

"Well, so you're Fenella," she said, and she gave the little girl a kiss. Fenella was not used to being kissed, and it warmed her heart. "I've heard about you from your Aunt Lou. You've come to help her, haven't you? She'll keep you at it all right!"

"Got anything to eat, Mum?" asked Willie. "I bet Fenella's hungry!"

"There's some buns in the cupboard there, and some strawberry jam somewhere," said Willie's mother.

"What's your mother's name?" whispered Fenella.

"Aggie," said Willie, giving Fenella a bun.

"I can't call her Aggie," said Fenella, shocked.

"Well, everyone does," said Willie. "You can call her *Aunt* Aggie, if you're so particular."

So Fenella called her Aunt Aggie, and she seemed quite pleased.

"Nice manners you've got," she said to Fenella. "And what pretty neat clothes you're wearing, too. Clever with your needle, aren't you? Wish I was. But I'm not. Can't even get myself to sew a button on! And as for Willie there, well, if he wants anything mending, he does it himself."

23

"I"ll do it for him," said Fenella, eagerly. "I'd like to. And I'll sew a button on your blouse for you, Aunt Aggie, and a hook on your skirt."

"There's no call to point out I've got safety pins where buttons ought to be!" said Aunt Aggie, looking suddenly offended. Fenella went red. But Willie nudged her and grinned.

"It's all right. Don't worry. Mum's never annoyed for long."

He was right. Before two minutes had gone by Willie's mother was rattling on about the circus, and how it was to open the next night, and what a good show they hoped to have.

"And my Willie here, he always gets the most claps, him and his old goose," she said.

"I don't, Mum!" said Willie, but his mother would have it that he did. The two of them finished their buns and jam, and then, with Cackles waddling beside them, Willie took Fenella round the camp to show her everything.

It was an astonishing walk for the little girl. She half-wondered if she was dreaming when she saw so many strange sights.

There were the three elephants, Dolly, Dick and Domo, in charge of a little man not much taller than Fenella herself.

"This is Mr. Tiny," said Willie, and the little man bowed gravely to Fenella. He was dressed all in white, with white boots and a white hat. "Just trying my things on for to-morrow night," he explained to Fenella. "Your aunt has made me some new ones. Do you like them?"

He swung himself round and round to show Fenella. "Fine, aren't they?" he said.

"You look lovely!" Fenella said, and the small man beamed. Beside his enormous elephants he looked tinier than ever. Fenella kept well away from the tremendous creatures.

"You needn't be afraid of them," said Mr. Tiny.

"They won't hurt you. Harmless as me, they are!"

He went up to Dolly, the smallest of the elephants. "Hup!" he said. "Hup!"

And Dolly put down her trunk, wound it gently round the waist of the little man, and set him on the top of her big head. Fenella was startled.

"Hup!" said Willie, too. "Hup!" And Dick, the next elephant, did exactly the same, winding his trunk round Willie's waist, and lifting the boy high up on his head.

"You say 'Hup!' to Domo!" called Mr. Tiny. "And he'll lift you up, too."

But Fenella backed away quickly. What! Be lifted up by an elephant's trunk and set on his head! She couldn't imagine anything she would hate more. Mr. Tiny and Willie laughed at her horrified face. Willie slid cleverly down to the ground.

"Come on! We'll see Mr. Holla. He's teaching his chimps to play cricket this year. It's funny to watch them."

"I'm afraid to go near the chimpanzees," said Fenella, pulling back.

"Don't be silly! You'll love them," said Willie. "See that one grinning at us? He's called Grin, and he's the wickedest, comicalest chimp you ever saw. There's the other, looking hurt and solemn. He's always like that. He's called Bearit. Grin and Bearit. Look out for Grin. He'll have the sweets out of your pocket if you're not careful."

Grin was like his name, one big grin. He showed very white teeth, and Fenella couldn't help feeling afraid of him. But he put out a gentle, hairy paw and stroked her arm softly, making a funny, loving little noise as he did so.

"He likes you!" said Willie. "He doesn't do that to many people, I can tell you. Here's their trainer, Mr. Holla. How are you getting on teaching your chimps cricket, Mr. Holla?"

Mr. Holla was a jolly-looking man, with long, powerful arms like his chimpanzees. They adored him. They liked nothing better than to put their hairy arms round his neck and hug him. Each chimpanzee was dressed carefully. Grin wore a pair of red shorts and a yellow jersey. Bearit wore a pair of yellow shorts and a red jersey.

"They've got caps, too," said Mr. Holla to Fenella. "But they were naughty with them yesterday, so I've taken them away for a punishment to-day."

"Oh. What did they do?" asked Fenella curiously.

"They wear caps," said Mr. Holla. "And Grin climbed up on top of your aunt's caravan yesterday and put his red cap on her chimney, and Bearit put his on Aggie's chimney. So both their stoves smoked and they were angry. And now to-day I won't let either of the chimps wear their caps, so maybe they won't do that again. They're full of tricks."

Grin had sidled up to Fenella. Somehow she couldn't help liking him. He looked so comical in his shorts and jersey, and he stroked her arm as if he thought she was the nicest little girl in the world.

Then he suddenly bounded off at top speed, with Bearit after him. He leapt up on to the top of Mr. Holla's van, which was nearby, and began to look at something he held.

"It's my sweets! " said Fenella indignantly. "He's taken them out of my pocket. And all the time he was stroking my arm and pretending to be so friendly."

"Well, you won't see your sweets again," said Mr. Holla. "They won't come down till they've eaten them all. Rascals they are. Worse than a dozen children! "

Mr. Holla went into his caravan and came out with an orange. "Here you are," he said. "You have that instead of your sweets. And don't be too cross with Grin and Bearit. Come and make friends with them some time. They love children."

A pack of dogs suddenly came rushing over to Willie.

The chimps sat munching Fenella's sweets

27

Fenella shrank behind him, but the dogs took no notice of her.

"Here are all the performing dogs!" said Willie to Fenella. "I help with them. This is Tric. This is Fanny. This is Corker. This is Bouncer. Will you get down, Buster! Stop it now! And leave my shoe-lace alone, Scamp. Aren't they lovely, Fenella?"

They were all so merry and full of fun that Fenella couldn't help liking them. Most of them were terriers, but there were two poodles and one mongrel.

"He's about the cleverest of the lot," said Willie, patting him. "Hup, Pickles, hup."

And up went Pickles on his hind legs at once, and then threw himself light-heartedly over and over in the air, somersaulting time after time. Fenella stared in wonder at him. But when Willie began to make a fuss of him, all the other dogs were jealous and came rubbing against Willie for some affection, too.

"Don't they love you!" said Fenella, and began to think it must be very nice to be so much loved by animals as Willie was. She held out her hand to one of the poodles, feeling very brave, meaning him to come and sniff at it, and perhaps lick it.

But the poodle very gravely put up his paw, too, and shook hands. Fenella laughed. "Oh, they're so clever. Who teaches them? Do they like being taught?"

"We only teach the clever ones," said Willie, "and they love it, of course—just as clever children enjoy their lessons. We never whip them—only reward them when they have done well. Now let's go and look at Mrs. Connie's monkeys."

He sent the dogs off and walked with Fenella to the other side of the field, where there were two caravans, both painted a bright green, with yellow wheels. Across each was painted "MRS. CONNIE AND HER MARVELLOUS MONKEYS."

Outside one of the caravans a tea-party was going on. Seven monkeys sat at a table, each on a small chair.

Each had a banana in his or her hand, and they watched a tiny, wizened woman, looking rather like a monkey herself, who sat at the head of the table. She was talking to them.

"Now Millie, now Minnie, now Mollie, remember your manners. Peel your banana neatly like this. That's right. Only peel it halfway, remember, Jimmy! You've taken your peel right off! Naughty, naughty!"

Jimmy looked like a bad child caught doing something wrong. He whimpered and tried to put the peel back on his banana. The others had half-peeled theirs and were patiently waiting for Mrs. Connie to let them bite a bit off the top. Fenella saw that each monkey had its own tiny mug with its name painted on it. How lovely!

Mrs. Connie suddenly saw them. "Hallo, Willie. Who's this? A friend of yours?"

"It's Fenella, who's come to live with her Aunt Lou," said Willie. A scowl came over Mrs. Connie's face.

"That Lou! Mean, selfish woman! She makes such a fuss when she has to sew something for my monkeys. Well, girl, I hope you're not as mean as your aunt, that's all. If you are, I'll have nothing to do with you. Nothing! Jimmy! Behave yourself! You've thrown your skin on the floor. Pick it up at once!"

Jimmy picked it up. Then, when the next monkey wasn't looking, he took a neat bite off the top of its banana. The monkey howled loudly and chattered to Mrs. Connie.

Fenella laughed and laughed. Mrs. Connie looked pleased. "Comical, aren't they?" she said. "Good as gold, really."

Fenella thought they looked sweet. Some were dressed in tiny skirts, others in tiny shorts. Willie pulled at her hand.

"Come on. There's lots more to see. Let Mrs. Connie get on with her tea-party. Well, do you like us all?"

"Oh, I *do*," said Fenella, her face glowing. "I do, Willie. I'm *so* glad I didn't run away!"

29

UNCLE URSIE'S BEARS

JUST as Fenella and Willie were leaving Mrs. Connie and her troupe of monkeys, Uncle Ursie saw them, and came up.

"Well, Fenella," he said, "making friends with everyone? Hallo, Cackles."

"Cackle," said the goose, and dug his beak affectionately into Uncle Ursie's boot.

"Hey, don't do that," said Uncle Ursie, and pushed the goose off. She hissed, and dug her beak into his leg.

"Too affectionate, that goose of yours," said Uncle Ursie, rubbing his leg. "Seen my bears yet, Fenny? What, not seen them! Come along then. Finest animals in the show! "

He took them to a big van, one side of which had been folded back. Bars were all along the open side, and at one end was a door. Uncle Ursie opened it and went inside.

A big brown bear stood up as he came in. Fenella had seen so many animals now that she actually didn't feel afraid. "Come and make friends with Fenny," said Uncle Ursie to the big bear.

"His name is Clump," said Willie. "He won't hurt you. Your uncle has had him since he was a baby. Hallo, Clump."

Clump grunted right down in the middle of himself. Fenella wasn't sure what she ought to do, so she put out her hand. But the bear put both his arms round her and gave her a hug. She gasped.

"Haven't you heard of a bear-hug?" asked Uncle Ursie, with a grin all over his face. "Clump, stand on your head."

Clump rolled over and then, to Fenella's surprise,

30

stood on his head. Then he turned three slow somersaults, and ended up sitting beside Uncle Ursie. He at
once put his arms round Uncle Ursie's knees and hugged
them.

"Stop it," said Uncle Ursie. "You'll crack my knee-
joints. Now then—where's Bobbo?"

Bobbo was asleep in the straw at the very back of the
cage. He awoke and yawned. Fenella stared at him,
and her heart went out to the little fat brown bear. He
was only a baby!

She forgot that she was ever afraid of animals. She
held out her arms for the dear little bear. Uncle Ursie
picked him up, and gave him to her. He cuddled into
her arms and stared up at her out of small, brown eyes.
He yawned again.

"Oh, you're a pet!" said Fenella. "Uncle Ursie, I
want to play with him every day. Oh, he's so cuddlesome
and soft. I'd like to take him to bed with me at night!"

"Ho! And I wonder what your aunt would say to
that!" said Uncle Ursie. "A bear in your bed, indeed.
Bobbo! Do you hear that? This little girl wants to
make you a pet and take you to bed."

"Ooof," said Bobbo, and rubbed his blunt nose with
one of his paws. Fenella really loved him. He was such
a baby.

"Does he go into the ring and do anything at all?"
she asked Uncle Ursie.

"He goes into the ring all right, but he doesn't do
anything yet. He's too young," said her uncle. "He
will watch Clump, and do what he does later on. He's a
comical little fellow. Maybe he'll be a kind of bear-
clown. Some bears are just naturally comical you know.
Willie, take that goose of yours out of the cage. One
blow of Clump's paw and that will be the end of her."

"Oh, Cackles can look after herself all right," said
Willie. "We had a tiger here once, and she gave him
a peck, because he lashed out with his tail and hit her
by mistake!"

It was getting dark now, and Uncle Ursie came out of the cage with the others. Fenella had to put down the baby bear. He grunted softly as if he didn't want her to leave him.

Uncle Ursie locked the cage. "Come along," he said to Fenella. "Supper-time. Then bed for you! You must be tired with your long day."

"She hasn't seen the horses yet, or Fric and Frac, the riders, or Malvina—and she hasn't seen Groggy, our old clown—or the others, Ricky and Rocky, and Micko and Tricks," said Willie. "And there's Wriggle, too, she hasn't seen."

"Yes, I've seen *him*," said Fenella. "He put his head between his knees and looked out at me from there. I didn't like it."

Willie laughed. "Oh, you'll have to get used to old Wriggle. He's got a body made of rubber. Wait till you see him tread on his head!"

"He couldn't!" said Fenella. "You're making that up. Oh, I wish I could see the clowns."

"They don't look any different from me or Willie here," said her uncle. "Not in ordinary dress, I mean. And they're not very funny out of the ring, either. Except old Groggy. You wait till to-morrow evening, Fenella, and you'll see them in the ring, all dressed up in their clown clothes. Then they'll look like clowns—and act like them, too. You'll be doubled up with laughter. Come along now, or your aunt will be shouting for us. Get along, Willie, and take that goose with you. The sight of her drives Lou mad, ever since she climbed into the caravan and ate all the salad she had got ready for our dinner."

"Cackle," said the goose, and walked away as if she was offended.

"Good night, Fenella," said Willie. "See you tomorrow. And don't you run away in the night, or I shall be very cross!"

Fenella laughed. No, she wasn't going to run away

32

now. She began to feel excited at the thought of sleeping in a caravan. She had never done that before. It would be fun.

She went up the steps into the brightly-lit caravan, followed by Uncle Ursie, who was sniffing loudly.

"Sausages, I declare! My, I'm hungry, too! And onions with them—and tomatoes. We're in luck."

At Auntie Janet's Fenella had never had any supper except a piece of bread and butter. But things were different at the circus. The circus folk liked good meals and plenty of them. There was always a cooking-pot smelling delicious at the back of somebody's caravan, or the smell of frying sausages or bacon. There was tinned fruit at nearly every meal—peaches or apricots, pears or pineapple.

Such things had been a Sunday treat at Auntie Janet's. The circus folk had to depend a good deal on tinned stuff, and they bought the tins by the dozen. Fenella was thrilled to see a tin of apricots open on the shelf—and goodness, was that a jug of cream?

It was. The little girl found that she was hungry and she sat down to her plate of sausages, onions and tomatoes with a good appetite. Whatever would Auntie Janet say if she saw her eating a supper like that?

She was very sleepy afterwards, but her aunt made her help with the washing-up. Fenella took a look at the corner where all the gay clothes had been, waiting to be mended. Her aunt saw her look.

"All done," she said. "Whilst you were out gadding this afternoon. There will be no more for a bit. Everything's ready for the circus to open to-morrow—but afterwards there'll be plenty to do again—rents and tears, buttons off, new dresses to make. You'll have to start work then."

"I'll be glad to help you, Aunt Lou," said Fenella.

"Well, we can't afford to keep you here with us, unless you do your bit," said Aunt Lou. "We're not rich folk, you know. Everybody has to turn to and help in a circus.

33

We're like one big family. You be a good girl and I'll be glad to have you. You be lazy and you'll get the sharp side of my tongue—and Uncle Ursie can tell you how sharp that is!"

Uncle Ursie grunted. "Sharp! It would go clean through a battleship that tongue of yours, once it gets going. You used to be such a sweet-tempered girl, Lou. Don't you be too hard on the youngster. She's all we've got, now Janet's gone away. She seems a nice enough kid."

"She might be worse," said Aunt Lou, and her voice was not quite so sharp. "She'll have to have some schooling, too, Ursie. Maybe we'd better ask Presto to teach her lessons, when he's got time. She's only ten."

"I can read and write and do sums," said Fenella. "And I know a lot of geography and history."

"Do you now?" said Uncle Ursie, in admiration. "Well, that's more than some of us know here in this circus. There's two or three can't even write their own names. Yes, I'll ask Presto to teach Fenella when he can. He's a good-hearted chap, and clever as paint."

"Who's Presto?" asked Fenella, with curiosity, for she hadn't heard of him yet.

"Presto? Oh, he's the juggler and conjurer," said Uncle Ursie. "Marvellous fellow. You'll have to be careful to do what he says, or he may use a bit of magic and turn you into a chimp!"

"Now don't tell such stories," said Aunt Lou. "Fenella won't want to learn from him if you say things like that. Maybe if she goes to lessons with him, that young limb of a Willie will go, too. He's not had any more schooling than a fly! I doubt if he can read properly yet."

Fenella was astonished to think that Willie might not be able to read. How dreadful! She had been able to read since she was five. She thought about Presto. Fancy having lessons from a conjurer! That really *would* be

34

exciting. He might do tricks for her, if she worked well. Living in a circus camp was going to be very exciting indeed.

"Get into your bunk, Fenella," said her aunt, letting down the little narrow shelf, and piling bedclothes on it. "Go and rinse your face and hands in the stream outside. The light from the caravan will show you where it is."

Fenella washed herself in the cold stream. She went back into the caravan, found her brush and comb and brushed her hair well. Aunt Lou watched her.

"You've nice hair," she said. "I had a little girl once with hair like yours. It used to shine like that when I brushed it."

"What happened to your little girl?" asked Fenella. "Did she die?"

"Yes," said Aunt Lou. "She fell ill, and I couldn't get a doctor in time. Now you get into bed, quick! You won't wake up till goodness knows when if you stay up any later. Hurry! "

She didn't offer to kiss Fenella. The little girl climbed into her bunk sleepily. "Good night, Aunt Lou," she said.

"Good night," said Aunt Lou, in her sharp voice, and threaded a needle to do some darning of her own. Fenella shut her eyes.

She heard the shouting of some of the circus folk outside. She heard the whinny of a horse, and the barking of two or three of the dogs. Then she heard the loud cackle of the goose, not far off.

"Willie's taking her round the field with him," she thought sleepily. "I like Cackles. And I like Willie and Willie's mother—and oh, that darling little baby bear, Bobbo! I love him! " And then she was fast asleep, and dreaming that she was wheeling Bobbo in her dolls' pram, with Cackles walking beside her!

THE FIRST MORNING

FENELLA slept soundly that first night in her aunt's caravan. She was so tired that she did not wake up until both her aunt and uncle were up and about, and having their breakfast. The smell of frying bacon awoke her.

She turned over in her little bunk and tried to think where she was. She looked up at the ceiling and saw all kinds of things hung there, and was astonished. Aunt Janet's ceiling had never had anything hung on it at all.

But, of course—this wasn't Aunt Janet's bedroom! This was Uncle Ursie's red caravan! She was in Mr. Carl Crack's circus! She was one of the circus folk now. Fenella felt her heart jump in excitement, and she sat up at once. Where did that smell of bacon come from? It was really a very nice smell indeed.

There was no one in the caravan. Fenella jumped out of her narrow little bunk and went to the open door at the back. She looked out on to the circus field, which was busy and crowded and full of noise. Circus folk got up early, and did many jobs before they had their breakfast. Horses, sleek and satiny, were already being cantered round the field by Fric and Frac the riders, and by a lovely girl, dressed in riding breeches, Malvina.

Fenella stood there in her nightdress, drinking in the sunny air and the lively scene. Her aunt, just below on the ground, saw her.

"So you're awake at last!" she said. "Come along down and have your breakfast, quick!"

"What! In my nightdress? Oh, I *couldn't*!" said

36

Fenella, quite shocked. She disappeared into the caravan to dress.

"Well, if you're so fussy, let your breakfast get cold," said Aunt Lou.

"Now, now," said Uncle Ursie. "The child has been nicely brought up by Janet. You let her keep her nice ways and good manners, Lou. Wouldn't you have wanted our own little girl to be like that?"

Aunt Lou said nothing. She put some bacon on a plate for Fenella, and covered it up to keep it warm. Very soon the little girl jumped down the steps. Uncle Ursie put his big clumsy arm round her.

"Well, it's nice to see you looking so perky and pleased with yourself. Now, you tuck into that bacon and then you can come and help me with the bears."

"She's got to help wash up and clean the caravan first," said Aunt Lou, in her sharp voice.

"Oh, of course I will," said Fenella at once. She knew already that she must do what Aunt Lou said before she did anything that Uncle Ursie suggested. If she didn't they would neither of them ever hear the end of it! Oh, dear—Aunt Lou was such a cross kind of person. What a pity!

Fenella watched the life of the circus going on round her as she ate. The dogs came tearing by, and Willie was with them. Behind waddled Cackles as usual. Where Willie went she was sure to go. The dogs kept well out of her way. They knew her sharp beak only too well.

"Hallo, Fenny! Sleep well?" called Willie. "Hey, Bouncer, will you come here! Tric, what are you doing? Drop that, Buster, drop it! You get plenty of good food without picking up any old rubbish!"

Horses whinnied by the stream, where they were being watered. Dolly, Dick and Domo suddenly trumpeted, making a tremendous noise, that made Fenella upset her tea in fright.

"Haven't you ever heard an elephant's voice before?"

said Uncle Ursie, mopping the tea off her frock with a big, red handkerchief. "You'll soon get used to it. They want their breakfast, you see. A cartful of hay they'll eat, all in a twinkling!"

"They use their trunks just like hands," said Fenella, forgetting to eat her bread and marmalade. "Look— they put their food into their mouths with their trunks. Uncle, are their trunks very, very long noses?"

"Looks like it!" said Uncle Ursie. "They must have grown longer and longer, because elephants like to reach up to pull down leaves from tall trees. Ho, ho! If my nose was much bigger than it is, I'd use it for a hand, too!"

"It *is* rather big, isn't it?" said Fenella, looking at her uncle's large nose. He wasn't a bit offended. He put up his hand and felt it.

"Yes, it's big enough—it's a snout like old Clump's, your aunt says. Don't you, Lou?"

"Let the child eat her breakfast," said Aunt Lou. "We're late as it is."

Fenella quickly finished her bread and marmalade. The early summer sunshine shone down on the camp, and in the distance the fields were golden with buttercups. From somewhere nearby came the sweet, rich scent of may-blossom. Fenella sniffed it eagerly. However could she have thought it would be dreadful to live in a circus? Why, it was the most exciting thing in the world! And already she was not nearly so much afraid of the animals.

She thought of Bobbo the baby bear. She would hurry up and help her aunt with the washing-up and cleaning, and then perhaps Uncle Ursie would let her play with the little bear. He was such a darling.

She helped Aunt Lou neatly and quickly. "I must say your Aunt Janet has brought you up well," said Aunt Lou, in a nicer voice than she had used to Fenella so far. "I can see you'll be quite a help to me, for all you're only ten."

"I mean to be, Aunt Lou," said Fenella. "It's so kind of you and Uncle Ursie to take me in, when I've got nobody else. Now can I go and see the bears?"

"Yes, off you go," said Aunt Lou. "But remember, Fenella, that to-day is a very busy one for us circus folk because we're giving our first show here this evening, and you'd best not get in anyone's way. Most of all keep out of Mr. Carl Crack's way. He's always in a temper the first day the show opens."

"Oh," said Fenella, rather alarmed. She made up her mind to run and hide if she saw Mr. Crack anywhere. She didn't want him to shout at her again, or crack that enormous whip round her feet.

The little girl made her way to where her uncle was cleaning out Clump's cage. The big bear was sitting outside on the grass, watching Uncle Ursie. He was chained to a tree-stump.

"Where's Bobbo?" asked Fenella.

"Oh, Willie's taken him for a walk," said Uncle Ursie. "Now just you bring me that clean straw over there, will you. No, not that, child, it's the dirty straw! We can't give old Clump dirty bedding. That's right."

Fenella looked round for Willie. She saw him at the other end of the big field, with Bobbo and Cackles. She sped off, nearly falling over Bouncer and Buster, two of the dogs, who were having a race all by themselves.

A small man in shorts and jersey was blowing up enormous balloons outside a caravan. They were beautiful ones, very big, and very gay. On each of them was printed a name. Fenella tried to see what it was.

"Mr. Groggy," was what she read. Yes, there it was on each balloon. "Mr. Groggy." So this small man in the funny little shorts must be Mr. Groggy, the chief clown. He didn't look a bit like one.

He saw Fenella staring at him and he looked up and winked at her. Then he screwed up his face in a most remarkable manner, and made a loud popping noise like a lot of balloons going bang. Fenella looked at him in alarm.

"That's what my balloons will do to-night in the ring," said Groggy, making his face look like itself again. "They'll go popping off. What a pity, what a pity!"

He got up to get some more balloons, and came back to his chair. He sat down and the chair doubled itself up under him. Groggy found himself on the ground. He got up and pulled his chair straight.

"Now don't you do that again!" he said to the offending chair. "Pretending you're too weak to bear my weight!" He sat down on it again, and once more the chair gave way and Groggy found himself on the ground. Fenella gave a squeal of laughter.

"That chair!" said Groggy, and he shook his fist at it. He straightened it again, and pretended to sit down on it suddenly. The chair remained as it was. Then the clown sat down again—and once more the chair buckled up and there was the clown sprawling on the grass!

Fenella laughed and laughed. Mr. Wriggle the acrobat came up, grinning. "Hallo! Is old Groggy showing you what that chair of his can do? Like to see me tread on my head, Fenella?"

"No, thank you," said Fenella hastily, looking at Mr. Wriggle's long, lean body. "I'm just going."

"Well, have one of my balloons before you go," said Mr. Groggy, and he handed her a big blue one. He sat down on his chair and again it sent him to the ground. Laughing to herself, Fenella ran over to join Willie.

"Oh, you've got Bobbo with you!" she said. "Let me carry him. Do let me! He's like a toy bear, so soft and cuddly."

"Well, let him walk a bit first," said Willie. "He always enjoys his morning walk. He likes seeing all the other animals. We always let the animals mix together as much as we can, so that they know one another and get used to their different smells. Bobbo loves to amble round."

Fenella walked round the field with Willie. Bobbo, on a lead, followed clumsily, his fat little body waddling along as slowly as Cackles. The goose liked Bobbo. She hissed softly as they went. "She's talking to him," said Willie. "Telling him this and that, like I tell you! "

"Everyone seems awfully busy this morning," said Fenella, skipping out of the way of two men hurrying along with a big bench. "Oh dear—what are all these men doing with those benches?"

"Getting ready for the show to-night," said Willie. "The big top's up. We've got to get the ring ready now and the seats for the people."

"What's the big top?" asked Fenella.

"The circus tent, of course, where the ring is," said Willie. "Come over and peep inside. Don't tell me you've never been to a circus! My, my—what an ignorant little girl you are! "

Fenella had never been taken to a circus in her life. She peeped inside the "big top" as Willie called the great centre tent. She saw a red ring in the middle of it, which two men were strewing with sawdust. Around the ring other men were setting dozens of wooden benches.

"Can I see the show to-night?" asked Fenella, in excitement. "Will Aunt Lou let me?"

"See the show! I should just think so," said Willie. "And mind you clap me and Cackles as loud as ever you can! My word, you'll enjoy yourself to-night! "

GETTING READY FOR THE SHOW

EVERYONE was busy and excited that day. Even the animals seemed to know that the circus was giving a grand show that evening. The elephants trumpeted dozens of times, the horses whinnied and neighed, the dogs barked, Cackles hissed and cackled, the bears grunted, and the monkeys chattered in little high voices. As for the chimpanzees, they were quite mad, and Mr. Holla had to speak to them very sternly indeed.

"What have they done?" asked Fenella, seeing Grin and Bearit putting their hands over their faces like children who have been scolded.

"Grin found a bucket of water and threw it all over Bearit," said Mr. Holla. "Soaked him through. Then Bearit got the empty bucket and tried to put it on Grin's head. And all the time Aggie was looking for her bucket of water. She *was* cross. So was I, when I saw Bearit's clothes dripping wet!"

Fenella laughed. The chimps took a look at her through their fingers, for their hands still covered their faces. Then Grin made a chattering noise and took her hand. She didn't mind at all.

"He likes you," said Mr. Holla. "He wants you to go for a little walk with him. I saw you with Bobbo in your arms this morning. Do you like him?"

"Oh, he's a darling," said Fenella. "And I like Clump, too—he's so fat and clumsy."

"Chimps are much better than bears," said Mr. Holla, half-jealously. "Got more brains in their feet that bears have in their big heads. You watch what Grin and Bearit do in the ring to-night! You'll be surprised."

Fenella watched everything and everyone that day, rather shy, but very thrilled to be part of the camp. She kept out of Mr. Crack's way. Indeed, everyone did if they possibly could, for he was strung up to such a pitch of excitement that he almost lost his voice through shouting orders all over the field. His whip cracked, his top-hat flew off twice in the wind, and he stamped about in his enormous boots like a giant!

"Don't you be afraid of him!" said Uncle Ursie, when he saw Fenella skip out of the way and hide under a caravan when Mr. Crack came roaring by. "He's always like that on show-days. Can't help it. He'll be all right afterwards."

Aunt Lou was now doing a few last-minute jobs that had turned up unexpectedly—a button to sew on to Malvina's beautiful costume—a tear to mend in Mr. Groggy's clown's dress—a black bobble to put on Micko's hat. Fenella offered to help, but her aunt shook her head.

"No," she said, her needle flying in and out, "I can do these few things. You go and watch the circus getting ready. Look at the gate over there—the people are already lining up to get in. They know that Mr. Carl Crack's circus is a fine one to see!"

"It's the best in the world!" said Fenella, making up her mind that it really must be. She watched the circus folk parading about, looking suddenly very different now that they had got on their beautiful, gay circus clothes. How grand they looked—and how very lovely Malvina was. She was one of the trick-riders, and when she came by Fenella looked in wonder at the glittering stars in her hair, and the smaller ones sewn on to her lovely dress.

The clowns were all dressed up now, too. Mr. Groggy looked extremely funny, for he had put on a false nose that was longer and bigger than even Uncle Ursie's. He had put big white rings all round his eyes, and painted his mouth red, making it most enormous. He carried his

43

bunch of big balloons, and also his peculiar chair.

The other clowns were ready, too, and Mr. Wriggle the acrobat was in a tight-fitting suit of shining gold. He saw Fenella and winked at her. "I wish you'd watch me tread on my head," he said in a pleading voice. "Look, I just do this—and . . ."

To Fenella's alarm he twisted himself over backwards and his head appeared under his left arm. She stared in horror.

"No, don't tread on your head. Don't do anything like that," she begged Mr. Wriggle. "I don't like it."

"Well, well, well! How do you like *this* then?" cried Mr. Wriggle, in a gay voice, and threw himself over on to his hands. He walked on them very fast indeed, his legs waving in the air.

"Oh, that's very clever," said Fenella. "*I'd* like to do that! Oh, here's Willie—and Cackles. Willie, you look FINE! And oh, doesn't Cackles look sweet?"

The goose looked like Mother Goose in the nursery rhyme books. She had on a dear little bonnet with a feather in it, and wore a red shawl. Under her wing she carried a shopping basket. She cackled as if she was very pleased with herself. Indeed, she was, because there was nothing she enjoyed better than dressing up with Willie and waddling after him in the ring.

Willie looked very grand indeed. He had on a shining white suit, with a cloak edged with bright red. His round, white hat had a red feather in it, very long and wavy. He looked quite a different boy.

"You look like a prince," said Fenella, admiringly. "Oh, Cackles—how *do* you carry your basket so nicely?"

"I clip it to her wing—look, there's the clip," said Willie, showing Fenella a big white clip that fastened the basket under Cackles' wing. "I say—here's your uncle. He wants you for something."

Fenella hardly knew her uncle at first when she saw him. He, too, had put on his grand circus clothes, and looked quite different. He wore Russian dress, with big

Cackles looked very handsome in her bonnet

top-boots, a red coat with a belt, red breeches tucked into his boots, and a tall, round black fur cap. His big nose seemed to suit him now. He smiled at Fenella.

"Well, how do you like us when we're properly dressed? Hold Bobbo for me for a minute, will you? He's getting so excited that he won't be able to do a thing when he gets into the ring."

Fenella held her arms out gladly for the little bear, who was whimpering with excitement. He sensed all the preparations, and felt all the eagerness of the hurrying circus folk, and it was too much for his baby mind. He cuddled against Fenella gladly.

"You're a darling," she said. "Don't shiver so, Bobbo. It's very warm to-night!"

"He's shivering with excitement, not cold," said Willie. "Some of the dogs get like that. They love all the thrill of the show. Bouncer gets so excited sometimes that he shivers from head to foot. But he's quite all right as soon as he gets into the ring."

Mrs. Connie passed by with her monkeys, and Fenella didn't know her! No wonder, for she had left off her old draggled skirt and shawl, and had dressed herself in a frilly skirt, short to her knees, and a gay little blue coat. She wore a bright golden wig, and was talking gaily to her little troupe of monkeys. Each of them was in his or her circus dress, and looked very smart indeed.

"Is that really Mrs. Connie?" said Fenella in amazement. "But she looks *young* now! And she looked awfully old before."

"Doesn't matter what you look like in the daytime, in the camp," said Uncle Ursie, "but at night, when the show is on, we must all be young and gay and strong. Look at the people pouring in now. We shall take a lot of money to-night. Mr. Crack will be pleased to-morrow."

"Where shall I sit?" asked Fenella. "In the front row of the seats? Oh, I do hope I can, then I shall see everything."

"In the *seats*! Don't be so silly," said Willie. "Fancy one of us in a *seat*! You'll be behind the curtains with us of course, Fenny. You'll see us all go in, in our turn. You belong to the circus now, you know."

A bell rang. All the circus folk still outside the big top hurried towards it. It was almost time for the show to begin. Hundreds of people were now in the great tent, waiting eagerly. The smell of animals rose on the air, and Fenella wrinkled up her nose. She would soon get used to that smell, and not even notice it. The town children, waiting impatiently on the benches in the big tent, smelt it too, and began to clap loudly, for they wanted the show to begin.

Fenella went behind the great red curtains that hung at one end of the tent, through which the performers appeared to do their turns. In the space beyond the curtains were the circus folk, the horses and other animals, all getting into order, and waiting impatiently for Mr. Crack to give the signal.

"We all parade round first," Willie told her. "Fric, Frac and Malvina go with a string of horses, and then Mr. Crack, in his golden carriage, drawn by Malvina's own six snow-white ponies. Then all of us, one after another."

Mr. Crack's voice rose above the noise. "Fric! Lead the parade."

And then, with a great blare of trumpets, Mr. Carl Crack's Stupendous Circus began. The big red curtains were swung aside, and through them cantered some of the magnificent circus horses, shining like satin, their proud heads tossing great plumes as they went.

Fric and Frac were dressed as Red Indians with great feathered head-dresses. Their faces were painted in brilliant colours, and they looked very grand and rather frightening. The children in the audience clapped and shouted wildly when they saw them. They thought they were real Red Indians. Fric and Frac gave some blood-

47

curdling yells as they rode round, guiding the string of horses.

Then came the six snow-white ponies, the foremost one ridden by the beautiful Malvina. They drew a shining coach in which sat a most resplendent Mr. Crack, bowing this way and that as everyone cheered him.

His carriage stopped. He got out, a big impressive figure, his whip in his hand. He took off his grey top-hat and bowed. He called out in a tremendous voice:

"Ladies and gentlemen—welcome to Mr. Carl Crack's Grand Circus. On with the SHOW!"

And then, tumbling over and over, came the clowns and Mr. Wriggle the acrobat, Mrs. Connie and her monkeys, Mr. Holla and his two chimpanzees, looking very fine in circus clothes. Mr. Tiny and the three elephants, Uncle Ursie and the bears, Willie and Cackles —the whole string of circus performers, dressed in their finest clothes, bowing and smiling, yelling delightedly at all the shouts and claps and stamps of applause.

Yes, the circus had begun—and to a little girl peering through the curtains, her heart beating fast, it was the most exciting moment of her life. Yesterday she had been a small girl all alone—now she was one of this big circus family. She belonged to them all and they belonged to her. What fun, thought Fenella, oh, what fun!

FENELLA SEES THE CIRCUS

THE circus was very fine indeed. After the parade, when everyone had walked or ridden round the ring, bowing and smiling, the show really began.

First came the horses, cantering beautifully one after the other, round and round the ring. They went in time to the music, and they obeyed Malvina's slightest word or nod. They turned themselves round and round, they waltzed, they made themselves form patterns, and they knelt on one knee and bowed their heads when they had finished.

The band played all the time, and Fenella couldn't imagine how the horses kept time—but they all loved music, and had been specially chosen because of their liking for it. The little girl clapped and shouted as loudly as anyone as the lovely horses cantered out of the ring, with Malvina standing on the back of the biggest.

Then one by one the other turns went on. The three elephants were an enormous success, for Mr. Tiny had taught them how to play tennis. He and Domo played against Dicky and Dolly. They had a net stretched across the ring, and they played quite properly with a tennis ball and rackets.

"Oh, Domo is very, very good!" said Fenella, watching him hit the ball hard with his racket, which he held firmly in his trunk. "Oh good, Domo! Well hit!"

Dolly hit the ball such a smack that it went right up to the ceiling and down again. It bounced high and Dicky lunged out with his racket in his trunk. "Smack." The ball flew into the delighted audience, and a small boy caught the ball and flung it back.

When the game was over Domo curled his trunk round his beloved Mr. Tiny and put him gently on his great

49

grey head. Mr. Tiny stood there, dressed in white from top to toe, a small, bowing figure. Everyone cheered wildly. Then out lumbered the big elephants, their trunks swaying to and fro.

"We're next," said a voice in Fenella's ear. She turned and saw Mrs. Connie, looking amazing in her bright golden wig. Her monkeys were riding in a small carriage! Two monkeys were the horses, the driver was a monkey with a whip, and the other four monkeys sat in the carriage as passengers. They looked really amusing, and were clearly enjoying the fun immensely.

The driver-monkey was so excited that he quite forgot himself as he drove into the ring, and stood up and did a little dance, cracking his whip round his head. The passenger-monkeys knew he shouldn't do that, and one of them tried to pull him down.

"Be good now, be good!" hissed Mrs. Connie. "Jimmy, stop dancing and sit down."

They had a tea-party in the ring and behaved most beautifully. Then, after that, in went the clowns, shouting and falling over each other, playing all kinds of ridiculous tricks, and popping poor Mr. Groggy's beautiful balloons whenever they could creep up behind him without being seen.

In despair he handed the rest of them to some of the children in the audience, who, of course, were simply delighted. "Look," they said to one another, "the balloons have got the clown's name on—Mr. Groggy— we've got some of his own balloons!"

Then turning cartwheels and somersaults over and over again the clowns rushed out shouting, to make room for Mr. Wriggle the acrobat. A tight-rope made of strong wire had been stretched across the ring whilst the clowns had been playing about, and Mr. Wriggle walked this lightly and easily. Fenella thought he was wonderful.

"*I* couldn't walk on a wire like that!" she said to Willie, who was nearby. "I should fall off. Oh, what's he doing now?"

Mr. Wriggle was now swinging to and fro on a little silver swing high up in the roof of the big tent.

"Suppose he falls?" said Fenella to Willie. "Will that net underneath catch him?"

"Yes. But he never falls—unless he means to! " said Willie, with a grin. "Sometimes he thinks he'll give the people a fright, and he pretends to be in difficulties, almost falling but not quite—and then he gives a frightful yell and lets himself drop. My word, it gives the people a scare, I can tell you! "

"Look at him holding by one foot and swinging! " cried Fenella. "Oh, I don't think I can watch him. I shan't! "

She turned away and looked behind her. There she saw an adorable little house, complete with a front path and a gate! On the gate was painted "Mother Goose's Cottage."

"Oh! " cried Fenella, "I haven't seen that before. Willie, is that what Cackles uses in the ring?"

"Yes," said Willie. "That's her house. Isn't it, Cackles? She stays in it till I call her out. I do a lot of bird imitating first, you know, before Cackles joins me."

"When do you go into the ring?" asked Fenella, eagerly. "Soon? I'm longing to see you. Are you nervous, Willie?"

"Nobody's ever nervous! " said Willie, scornfully. "We've lived all our lives in the circus. Most of us were born in one. Why should we be nervous? Hallo—it's my time to go on."

Out came Mr. Wriggle, bowing as he came backwards through the curtains. Into the ring went Mr. Crack, with his big whip, to announce Willie.

"And now, ladies and gentlemen, we present to you Willie Winkie the Wonderful Whistler. He will imitate for you all the birds of the air, and will introduce to you Cackles, the trained goose, the only goose in the world who goes shopping! "

He cracked his whip. The trumpets shrilled out and

in ran Willie, looking beautiful in his shining suit and red-bordered cloak. Uncle Ursie carried in the little Mother Goose Cottage, helped by Fric and Frac. They set it down carefully, hearing a warning hiss from inside. Cackles was already there, behind the little front door, waiting for the time to appear.

Willie was really wonderful. He whistled and fluted, and it seemed as if the circus tent must be full of calling birds. He put his hands to his mouth and blew through his thumbs, making a hooting noise just like an owl. From somewhere outside the tent an owl answered him.

The audience were so quiet that everyone heard the answering owl. Then Willie sang like a nightingale in the night. It seemed impossible that a boy could make such natural bird-sounds. When he bowed low, to right and left, everyone clapped madly. "Encore!" they cried. "Encore!"

Willie waited for silence. Then he made other bird noises. He clucked like a hen. He crowed like a cock, he gobbled like a turkey, he quacked like a duck.

The children roared with laughter. And then Willie cackled like a goose! That was Cackles' signal to come out. Before the surprised and delighted eyes of hundreds of watching children and their parents, the little front door of the small cottage opened, and out walked Cackles herself!

She had her bonnet on nice and straight, and her shawl was very neat. Under her wing she carried her shopping basket.

She walked down the little front path and with her beak she opened the catch of the gate. Out she went into the ring.

And now Willie was behind a little stall on which were set butter, eggs, lettuces and other things. Willie had taken off his feathered hat and put on a shopkeeper's white cap. He had tied an apron round his waist—he was a shopkeeper!

Cackles walked solemnly up to him.

"Cackle, cackle, cackle," she said.

"A pound of butter, Madam? Certainly!" said Willie, and handed her a packet of butter. The big goose took it in her beak and put it carefully into her basket.

"Cackle, cackle," she said again.

"An egg? Yes, Madam. New-laid to-day!" said Willie, and handed her an egg. The goose was very careful with it. She put that into her basket, too.

"Cackle, cackle, cackle," she said to Willie.

"A nice fresh lettuce? Here you are, Madam. That will be two shillings altogether," said Willie. The goose took a purse out of her basket with her beak and handed it to Willie. He took money from it and gave it back to Cackles, who put both purse and lettuce carefully into her shopping basket.

"Cackle," said Cackles, and walked away.

"Good day, Madam," said Willie. Cackles walked solemnly to her little front gate. She bowed her head gracefully to left and right, undid the gate, shut it, and walked up the little path. She undid the front door, walked in, and slammed it shut.

Then what a clapping there was! What a shouting and stamping! Willie bowed dozens of times, delighted, and then ran off. Cackles came out of her little house and waddled after him, cackling loudly.

"Oh, Willie, Willie, you were marvellous! And so was Cackles!" cried Fenella, still clapping hard as the two of them came through the curtains. "Oh, wasn't Cackles wonderful? I'd no idea she could do all that."

"I taught her myself," said Willie proudly.

"Isn't he fine?" said Willie's mother, who had been watching Willie through the curtains, too. She looked drab and plain in her ordinary clothes, beside all the glittering gaily-dressed circus performers. Her lovely smile lighted up her face as she looked proudly at Willie. Fenella smiled, too. Willie was her friend, and she was very, very proud to have somebody so clever for a friend.

The clowns went on again, Mr. Groggy with a fresh supply of balloons. Then Fric and Frac went on to do some trick-riding with their horses. Then came the performing dogs, yelping madly with joy. The two poodles and the mongrel were the cleverest. One poodle could turn somersaults in a most remarkable manner.

"But once he starts he's difficult to stop!" said Willie. "He gets sort of wound up. Ah, he's stopped now. Now they're going to play football. Hark at the yells!"

Every dog got a big biscuit as a reward, and carrying them jealously in their mouths, they tore off through the red curtains to eat their tit-bits in some safe corner. Fenella sighed with excitement. She hadn't known that such a world as this existed. And to think she would be able to see all this again and again and again.

The two chimpanzees were a great success, and so was Presto the juggler and conjurer. Uncle Ursie and his bears got as many claps as anyone. There was not a poor turn in the whole circus. Everyone put up a good show and when the circus folk and their animals paraded themselves once more round the ring, to bring the performance to an end, the audience stood up and cheered so loudly that Fenella had to put her fingers in her ears!

"How they've all enjoyed it!" she said to little Bobbo the bear, who was half-asleep in her arms. "But who do you think enjoyed it most of all, Bobbo? I did! I really, really did!"

THE NEXT DAY

THE circus show was over. The people who had come to see it were streaming over the field towards the gate, to catch buses that stood there waiting.

"Wonderful!" they said. "Best show we've ever seen! We'll come again. My, weren't those elephants good?"

The three elephants were taken by Mr. Tiny to sleep under a big tree. It was hot that night, so they would be glad to sleep out of doors. Domo trumpeted and that started all the rest of the excited circus animals making their various noises, too. They were like children, easily excited by one another, eager to join in everything that went on.

The chimpanzees were taken off to Mr. Holla's big caravan. Fenella followed curiously, wanting to see where they slept. She peeped inside Mr. Holla's caravan, and saw two bunks there, one on each side, both made ready for sleeping in, with sheets, blankets and pillows.

"I sleep in this bunk," said Mr. Holla. "And Grin and Bearit sleep together in the other. They curl up in each other's arms. Grin snores sometimes, but otherwise they are very good at night."

"Who dresses them in the morning?" asked Fenella.

"They dress themselves," said Mr. Holla. "I've had them since they were babies, you know, and I've taught them just like you teach children. They even clean their teeth."

"Oh, *do* they?" said Fenella, amazed. "I *would* like to see them do that."

"Grin! Where's your toothbrush?" said Mr. Holla. Grin pounced on a small toothbrush and waved it at Mr. Holla, showing his teeth in his usual wide grin.

"Use it," commanded Mr. Holla, and Grin rubbed the brush over his teeth.

"Isn't he clever?" said Fenella. Grin was pleased with her praise and at once began to brush his hair, or rather the fur on his head. But as he did it with his toothbrush it didn't make much difference to it!

"You don't brush your hair with your toothbrush, Grin," said Mr. Holla in disgust.

"Fenella! Where are you?" suddenly called Aunt Lou's voice. "Now where has that child gone?"

"I'm here, Aunt Lou," cried Fenella. "Oh, don't say I've got to go to bed. I do feel so excited."

"We're all going to have a meal first," said Aunt Lou. "Then you must certainly go."

It was fun having that meal, so late at night. Each caravan had its own camp-fire burning brightly outside, whilst soup heated over the flames, or a frying-pan sizzled with bacon or sausages. Fenella was too excited to eat anything except some pineapple and custard. She sat on the step of her uncle's caravan, and watched the little camp-fires burning here and there in the dark blue of the night.

Someone began to play a banjo. "That's Micky or Tricks, I expect," said Uncle Ursie. The tune was jerky and jolly, and one or two of the circus folk began to sing it in low voices. Fenella yawned. She would have liked to sit there the whole night and watch the fires and hear the twanging of the jolly banjo, but her eyes were shutting all by themselves.

"Get into your bunk quickly," said Aunt Lou, giving her a push. "Go along now. You're not used to these late hours. You'll have to go to bed early when we go on the road to our next show-place."

"Oh, do we go to other places?" asked Fenella. "I hadn't thought of that. Goodness, how exciting it will be to move off to somewhere else. How long are we staying here?"

"Two more weeks," said Uncle Ursie. "This is a good

place for a circus. There are plenty of biggish towns nearby that will send people to see us. But we must move on in two weeks. Go into the caravan now, Fenny. You're yawning your head off."

Fenny went up the steps. She thought she would never be able to go to sleep because her mind kept seeing again and again all the things that happened in the ring. But no sooner was her head tucked into her pillow than she was fast asleep. She did not stir or wake till late in the morning—so late that Aunt Lou had cleared away the breakfast, washed up, and cleaned the caravan!

Fenella looked round the spotless caravan. Uncle Ursie was whistling just outside. Fenella called to him.

"Uncle Ursie! Am I very late waking up?"

"Well, it's nearly dinner-time, Fenella!" said Uncle Ursie, with a chuckle. "But never you mind. It's good for youngsters to sleep all they can. Makes them grow. Your aunt said if you wanted anything to eat, there's some cake in the cupboard there, and she's left you some egg sandwiches as well. There's some milk there too."

"Uncle Ursie, have you done the bears?" asked Fenella, dressing quickly. "I wanted to help you with Bobbo again."

"Yes, I've done them," said Uncle Ursie. "But you can take Bobbo for his walk, if you like, when you've had something to eat. Keep him away from the chimps though, because they'll tease him."

Fenella ate some breakfast, sitting on the steps of the red caravan. There was the usual noise and bustle in the camp. Willie was nowhere to be seen.

"He's gone to the hills with the dogs, taking them for a really good long walk," said Uncle Ursie. "He's a good boy, Willie is—always giving a hand with something."

"Oh—I do wish I hadn't waked up so late," said Fenella. "I'd have liked to go with Willie and the dogs."

"You can go plenty of other times," said Uncle Ursie.

"Are you ready to get Bobbo? Come along then, we'll get him."

Bobbo was delighted to see Fenella, and waddled over to her, making little grunting noises. Uncle Ursie was very pleased.

"You see if you can't teach Bobbo to do a few tricks for you," he said. "He's going to be a very clever little fellow."

"Oh, I couldn't teach him anything!" said Fenella. "I wouldn't know how to. But I love him. I never, never thought I'd love a real live bear—but this one's like a toy one, so cuddly and sweet."

She carried Bobbo back to the caravan with her. She set him down for a moment and then went into the van and fetched out Rosebud, her best doll. She showed her to Bobbo.

Bobbo looked solemnly at the doll. He didn't understand what it was. But somebody else did! There came an excited little chattering noise, and down from the roof of the next caravan bounded Millie, one of Mrs. Connie's monkeys. She sat herself on Fenella's knee and put out a little brown paw to Rosebud, touching her gently.

Fenella was startled to have the monkey jump on to her knee. She didn't know whether to be afraid or not. The monkey looked up at her with dark brown eyes, and made its little chattering noise again. Then it patted Rosebud on the cheek.

"Your paw is just like a tiny brown hand," said Fenella, and took it into her hand. She opened the funny little fingers. Millie stared at her—but it was the doll that the monkey had come to see.

Rosebud wore a blue bonnet with little pink roses stitched on each side, over the ears. Millie the monkey pulled the string and the bonnet came undone. In a trice the monkey had whipped it off, and had leapt in one bound to the top of the caravan.

"Chitter-chitter-chatter!" said Millie, and put the bonnet on her own head!

"Oh!" cried Fenella, "you naughty little thing! Give me back Rosebud's bonnet at once!"

But Millie took no notice. She had never had such a pretty bonnet in her life! She took it off and looked at it. Then she put it on again, this time back to front. She looked very quaint and comical. Fenella couldn't help laughing. She went into the caravan with Rosebud and Bobbo, who had to be helped up the steps, because he was so round and fat. Fenella put Rosebud into her bunk and covered her up.

Millie the monkey, wondering where Rosebud had gone, let herself carefully down the side of the caravan and peered in at the open window. How she liked that doll! She waited till Fenella had gone out again, and then she swung herself in through the window, still with the doll's bonnet on her head.

She went over to the bunk, and turned back the cover, looking at Rosebud. The doll had her eyes shut now, because she was lying down. Millie touched her eyelashes gently. Then she began to chatter to the doll.

Fenella was outside, looking for the naughty monkey. She saw her aunt coming up with a big shopping basket, and went to meet her. "I'll take that for you," she said. "Look at Bobbo, Aunt Lou. He's made such friends with me."

Her aunt went into the red caravan and Fenella followed her with the basket. Bobbo tried to clamber up the steps after them.

Aunt Lou gave a scream. "Look at that monkey—with your doll's bonnet on, Fenella! Now what did you let that tiresome creature in here for? I won't have animals in my caravan. I'm not like Mr. Holla, wanting to have them sleeping inside with me, nor yet like Mrs. Connie, wearing them round her neck, the silly creature!"

"Oh, Aunt Lou—I didn't know that the monkey was . . ." began Fenella, surprised.

Millie leapt to the top of the cupboard, knocking over a jug that was stood there. It fell and broke. Aunt Lou gave an angry cry. "Look at that! I've told Mrs. Connie time and again she ought to keep her monkeys with her. Letting them loose like this—and you inviting them into my caravan and dressing them up in your doll's clothes. You're a naughty girl."

"But Aunt Lou!" began poor Fenella again, almost in tears, "I didn't——"

"You take that monkey back to Mrs. Connie and tell her if I catch it loose again I'll not make a single thing more for any of her troupe!" cried Aunt Lou. "You tell her that!"

"Oh, I couldn't say that," said Fenella, crying. Her aunt gave her an impatient push. "Do you want a slap?" she said. "Do as you're told. Ah—now I've got you, you wicked little monkey! Here, Fenella, take it, and mind you deliver my message, or I'll lose my temper!"

Aunt Lou had lost her temper already, it seemed to poor Fenella. She took the chattering monkey and made her way out of the caravan, tears running down her cheek. How could she give a rude message to Mrs. Connie? Her Aunt Lou oughtn't to make her say things like that!

AUNT LOU IN A TEMPER

FENELLA, with the monkey in her arms, and the little bear Bobbo behind her, made her way to Mrs. Connie's caravans. Mrs. Connie herself lived in one, and her monkeys had the other.

Mrs. Connie was busy doing some washing. She didn't look a bit nice, as she had done in the ring the night before. Her bright golden wig was put carefully away in its box, the frilly skirt and little blue coat were hanging in the caravan. Mrs. Connie looked the little old wizened woman that she was.

She looked up at Connie with brown eyes very like Millie the monkey's. "Hallo," she said, "where has that little monkey been? Not in mischief, I hope."

"Well—he came into my aunt's caravan," said Fenella. "He saw my doll Rosebud there, you see—and—and— well . . ."

"And that sour-faced, sharp-tongued aunt of yours lost her temper with you and the monkey. I suppose, and packed you off with Millie?" said Mrs. Connie, guessing quite right.

"Yes," said Fenella. "She—she doesn't seem to like your monkeys very much, Mrs. Connie."

"I suppose she sent me a rude message?" said Mrs. Connie, rinsing her soapy clothes out over the grass. "Oh, go on—you can tell me what it is. I'm used to her rude ways. All because she doesn't like using her needle to dress my little ones! "

"She just said—that if you didn't keep your monkeys with you she wouldn't make any more clothes for them," said Fenella, going red.

"Ho, she did, did she? Well, you go back and tell her that if she will sew herself a nice new face, with a bit of a smile on it, and put a cheerful, kindly tongue into her mouth instead of the one she's got, I'll keep my monkeys under lock and key with pleasure! " said Mrs. Connie, losing her temper very suddenly, in a way she had.

"Oh—I couldn't possibly say that," said Fenella, in alarm. Taking rude messages from one person to another was dreadful. Whatever would Aunt Lou say to Mrs. Connie's message!

Mrs. Connie looked Fenella up and down with scorn.

"I expect you're like your aunt—turning up your nose at this and that—nagging and scolding. How your poor uncle stands that tongue of hers is more than I can make out. He must be a poor worm!"

Aunt Lou suddenly appeared round the side of the caravan. She had heard what Mrs. Connie said, and her mouth looked more screwed-up than ever.

"Not one more thing do I make for those smelly monkeys of yours, Mrs. Connie!" she burst out. "Not one! And you can go to Mr. Carl Crack a dozen times, if you like, and complain. I'm not making anything more for them!"

"Smelly! They're not smelly!" cried Mrs. Connie, in a rage. "Don't they get bathed every week, and brushed twice a day! Ho, you don't know what you're talking about. Smelly, indeed! What about Ursie's bears?"

Fenella began to cry. She wasn't used to upsets like this. Mr. Holla, who was nearby, strolled up with a smile on his face. He patted Fenella on the shoulder.

"Now don't you get upset," he said kindly. "They're always at it, these two, hammer and tongs. You go off to Willie—look, he's back again with the dogs—and take Bobbo with you. He likes the dogs."

Fenella wiped her eyes and went off. Oh, dear! Why did Aunt Lou have such a bad temper? Would she really not make any more things for the monkeys? Surely if Mrs. Connie complained to Mr. Carl Crack, he would fly into a fearful rage too, and crack his whip all over the place!

She ran to meet Willie. The dogs greeted her joyously, jumping up at Bobbo and trying to lick him. He screwed himself up in Fenella's arms, and looked with surprised eyes at the noisy little creatures below him.

Mr. Crack appeared from a very grand caravan. It was not a horse-drawn one like the others, but one that could be pulled by a car. Behind the van was Mr. Crack's magnificent car. Willie had already shown it to Fenella.

The little girl turned to run when she saw him, for she was still scared of him. But he put out a big hand and pulled her to him. He was smiling all over his big face. His shaggy eyebrows did not look so fierce as usual.

"Now what do you want to run away from me for?" he asked, putting his hand into his pocket. "You're Fenella, aren't you? That's a nice name. And here's something nice for you, because I can see you're a good little girl."

He put a bag of big, round peppermints into her hand. Fenella thanked him shyly. She didn't know what to think of the broad, giant-like man, roaring like a lion one minute, and kindly as a big dog the next. He gave her a bear-like hug.

"I like little girls. You come and tell me if anything goes wrong with you, and I'll put it right. That's what they all do in this circus. Nobody's really afraid of Mr. Carl Crack! Are they, Willie Winkie?"

"Well, sir," said Willie, hesitating, because he knew that he himself felt very scared of Mr. Crack when he was in a temper. And many a time he had skipped out of the way of that big, curling whip, which could give a nasty nip when Mr. Crack liked!

But Mr. Crack was in a very good temper that morning, and nothing could make him do anything but smile. The show had been a marvellous success last night, and much money had been taken. It looked as if the next nights would be as good. So Mr. Crack had left his whip behind him in his lovely caravan, and was going about with smiles all over his face.

Fenella and Willie went off with the bag of peppermints. "I shan't let those chimps near me till I've finished these sweets this time," she told Willie. "Have one? Oh, look, Willie, Bobbo wants one, too!"

"He likes anything sweet," said Willie. "No, don't waste them on the dogs, Fenny. They'll only spit them out. And don't give any to Cackles in case she chokes."

63

Fenella squealed as Domo squirted water over her

Fenella told him about the quarrel between her aunt and Mrs. Connie. "Oh, don't you worry about that," said Willie. "They're always squabbling, those two. The only thing is—Mrs. Connie gets over her temper quickly, but your aunt doesn't. I'm afraid she'll give you the rough side of her tongue all day. You come and have dinner with me and my mother if she's too bad. Aggie understands."

"It sounds funny to me, you calling your mother Aggie," said Fenella.

"Well, Mum then," said Willie. "Come on, let's put the dogs away, and we'll go and watch the elephants having a bathe in the stream."

Dicky, Dolly and Domo were very funny when they had their bathe. It wasn't really a bathe because the stream was small and the elephants enormous. What they did was to put their trunks down into the water, and take in as much as they could—and then up went their trunks and they squirted the cool water all over their backs!

"Oh! I never knew elephants could do *that* before!" said Fenella in delight. Then she gave a squeal, because Domo had turned towards her, and was squirting water all over her! She ran behind a tree, shaking the drops from her dress, and laughing.

The elephants had a fine time. They seemed to enjoy paddling in the stream, and they squirted water over themselves till they were thoroughly wet. Then Mr. Tiny led them back to their tree. Domo, seeing Bobbo the bear wandering under his feet, put his trunk down, picked the tiny bear up gently and set him on his head!

Bobbo gave a frightened grunt and Fenella gave a scream. "Oh, he'll fall, he'll fall! Mr. Tiny, quick, make him take Bobbo down. He'll fall!"

But Bobbo didn't fall, because the big, gentle elephant held him on safely with his trunk all the time. He looked at Fenella out of his wise elephant eyes, and

65

C

seemed to say, "What! Did you really think I would let Bobbo fall?"

Fenella went back to her aunt's caravan when it was dinner-time. She peeped inside. Aunt Lou looked very grim indeed.

"Oh, so you're back again, are you?" she said in her sharpest voice. "Playing about all morning, and then coming back to see what I've got for your dinner. You'll start work to-morrow, my girl. Wasting your time like this!"

"Aunt Lou, I——" began Fenella. But Aunt Lou would never let anyone get a single word in, once she had started scolding.

"And don't you go near Mrs. Connie or her monkeys," she went on. "She's a mean, disagreeable, lazy woman. And I mean what I said—I'll not make a single thing more for those monkeys of hers, not one! Let her thread a needle herself for a change, and set to work. Do her good!"

"Aunt Lou, may I go and have dinner with Willie?" asked Fenella timidly, trying to get a few words in.

"Oh, go if you want to," said Aunt Lou in a sour voice. "But you come back this afternoon and do a bit of washing for me."

"Oh yes, aunt," said Fenella and escaped thankfully down the steps. She ran across the field to where Willie's caravan stood. Cackles was outside, squatting on the grass. Willie poked his head out of his caravan window.

"Come to have dinner with us?" he asked. "I thought you would! I know old Lou when she's in one of her moods. Come on in."

Fenella had a good meal with Aunt Aggie and Willie. "Shall I help to wash up?" she said afterwards.

"Oh, no," said Aunt Aggie. "Willie will take the things down to the stream and rinse them for me. If you want to do something, Fenella, you could sew some buttons on his shirt for me! 'Tisn't that I can't do it—

but I just seem to put it off and off. You do it, there's a good girl."

"Of course I will!" said Fenella, and went to work with a will. Willie took a tray of dishes out to the stream and rinsed them clean. Cackles went with him, pecking at the bits left on the plates. Willie whistled like a blackbird as he worked, and two blackbirds flew down beside him in wonder.

"Clever boy, isn't he, my Willie?" said Aunt Aggie to Fenella. "Just like his father! Have you finished putting those buttons on? Oh, and you've mended that hole, too. My, you're a neat one with a needle! Your Aunt Lou will be glad of your help, I know."

"I think I'll go now, Aunt Aggie," said Fenella, getting up. "Thank you for my nice dinner. I've got to do something for Aunt Lou now, so I'd better go."

She sped over to her own caravan. Aunt Lou was sitting outside, sewing. "So here you are!" she said, in a nicer voice. "Well, go and get that bit of washing from the caravan, and do it for me. And to-morrow, as I said, Fenella—you'll start work properly, and no mistake about it!"

WILLIE DOESN'T WANT LESSONS

THE bustle and excitement of the evening's show began all over again about tea-time. The circus folk once more shed their drab, rather dirty old clothes, and put on their finery. Such sparkling dresses, such shining suits, such sweeping feathers and gay colours!

Nobody would ever think they were the same people who had wandered here and there over the camping field in the day-time.

Fenella watched them all coming from their caravans, and wished that she, too, had a beautiful dress to wear in the ring. She began to plan one for herself. Then she shook herself. "How silly I am!" she thought. "I shall never go into the ring like Willie. So I shall never need a gay glittering frock. But oh, how nice it would be to look like a princess every evening!"

Mrs. Connie appeared in her golden wig and frilly skirt. Her monkeys were all dressed in their pretty, gay ring costumes. Fenella wondered if her aunt had made them. Certainly she had made them beautifully, if so. Fenella began to think of other frocks and suits for the little monkeys. A little red soldier suit for Jimmy would be lovely!

Mrs. Connie waved to Fenella, but the little girl didn't dare to smile and wave back, because her Aunt Lou was nearby. She felt sure she would get a hard slap if she did!

Then once again the show began, and Fenella stood behind the big, red curtains, hearing the people shout and clap, watching the performers doing their clever turns.

Presto the juggler and conjurer was very skilful indeed. He could juggle with twelve balls at once, keeping them going up and down in the air, catching them and throwing them up again, never missing once. His conjuring was marvellous, too, and Fenella couldn't imagine how he could take so many yards and yards of coloured ribbon out of his mouth!

She looked at him shyly as he came out. This was the man who was to teach her and Jimmy. Did he look cross or impatient? She knew she would be afraid of him if so, because Fenella could not bear loud voices or cross looks.

Presto did not look cross or impatient. He looked

rather sad. He had never smiled once in the ring, even when the cheering people had yelled "Encore! encore!" at the tops of their voices. He stalked through the curtains, solemnly, his long, black cloak, lined with bright scarlet, sweeping behind him. He was a tall, thin man, with piercing dark eyes, and hair as black as night. He wore in the ring the tall, pointed hat, set with brilliant stars, that enchanters or wizards are supposed to wear.

"He looks a bit frightening," whispered Fenella to Willie, who was standing beside her with Cackles. "I wish we hadn't got to learn lessons with him, Willie."

Willie had heard about this idea from his mother and he wasn't at all pleased. He wrinkled up his freckled nose in dismay.

"Fancy having to waste time learning *lessons*! I've never been to school. Have you, Fenella?"

"Oh yes, of course I have," said Fenella. "I thought everyone had to go to school. How did you learn anything if you didn't go, Willie?"

"Oh, Mum taught me a bit—but she doesn't know much herself, really," said Willie. "And once we had a nice tight-rope walker called Anna, and she helped me a lot. We can't very well go to school properly, us circus children, because we're always moving on from place to place, you see."

"Can you read?" asked Fenella. Willie went rather red.

"Course I can," he said. "Don't be silly."

A loud burst of clapping told them that Uncle Ursie was coming out with his bears. Through the red curtains he came, bowing low, with Clump and Bobbo. Bobbo saw Fenella and went to her at once, getting a hard peck from Cackles because he pushed against her! But Bobbo didn't mind. His fur was much too thick to feel anything like that!

"Fancy being able to see all this every evening!" sighed

Fenella in delight. "I shall never, never get tired of it, Willie."

"Oh, it will seem quite ordinary to you after a time," said Willie laughing. "It's all so new, isn't it? You wait till you've been with the circus for a month or two— why, you won't even bother to come and peep through these red curtains then! You'll go to bed early, and sleep soundly in your caravan, whilst we're doing the show."

"I shan't!" said Fenella, indignantly. "I shall always, always want to see you all doing your turns—especially you and Cackles, Willie, and Uncle Ursie and the bears. I do think Clump is clever the way he turns head over heels."

"Did you notice one of the dogs in the ring to-night?" said Willie. "He wouldn't stop turning somersaults, he was so excited. And even when we all played football he went on turning head-over-heels without stopping. He always does that when he's excited."

Fenella was glad to tumble into bed again that night. "Work to-morrow!" she thought. "Lessons with Presto. Or do I call him Mr. Presto? Is that his real name, I wonder? All the circus people seem to have such queer names. And I shall have to start on some sewing with Aunt Lou, too—mostly mending, I suppose. But there will be new dresses to make after this show, I expect. I shall like that. I wish I could make a suit for Bobbo. Oh, wouldn't he be sweet all dressed up! But perhaps he wouldn't like it. The monkeys love it, so do the chimps."

She fell asleep. She didn't wake up quite so late the next day, as she had done the morning before, and was actually in time to have some breakfast.

"Have you spoken to Presto about the children?" asked Aunt Lou, as Uncle Ursie got up to go to his beloved bears.

"Yes. He's quite willing. He's got books and pencils, he says," said Uncle Ursie. "Fenella and Willie are to go at ten o'clock this morning."

70

"Uncle Ursie! Is he kind?" asked Fenella, anxiously. "He looks so sort of—well, solemn and sad you know."

"I've never seen him smile, now I come to think of it," said Uncle Ursie, rubbing his big nose, trying to remember a smile of Presto's. "No, not even when Grin got hold of Mrs. Connie's golden wig and put it on his own head. We all laughed fit to kill ourselves—but Presto just looked as solemn as ever."

"He's very clever," said Aunt Lou. "He can speak Latin and Greek. He's a gentlemanly fellow, too—not really one of us. He's a good teacher, though, Fenella, so you learn all you can from him. And see that Willie goes regularly, if you can. It's really time that boy could read properly."

"He says he can," said Fenella in surprise. "And he's so very, very clever, I'm sure he'll be better at everything, and beat me easily."

"Well, you'll see," said Aunt Lou. "Now you've just got time to help me clean the caravan, Fenella, then you go over to Presto's caravan. And this afternoon I want you to help me with the mending. It seems as if everyone in the show last night tore a hole in their clothes or ripped a button off!"

Fenella went to find Willie just before ten o'clock. He was giving Cackles a paddle in the stream. She loved that.

"Oh, Willie, it's time to come to Presto," said Fenella anxiously. She hated being late for anything.

"I'm not coming," said Willie.

Fenella stared at him in dismay. "Why not?" she asked. "Oh, Willie—I can't go alone!"

"I don't want to come," said Willie, not looking at Fenella at all. "Waste of time, that's what it would be. Can't I earn my own living, and help to keep my mother, too? Don't we get on all right without lessons? I'm not coming."

Fenella's eyes filled with tears. She was very dis-

71

appointed. Lessons without Willie wouldn't be any fun at all.

"Willie, I don't want to go without you," she said in a very small voice. "Do come."

"Why do you bother to go yourself?" said Willie, sounding rather scornful. He splashed Cackles all over with water, and the goose cackled in delight.

"Well, you know I've got to," said Fenella. "Aunt Lou would scold like anything if I didn't. I daresay she'd slap me, too. And anyway, Willie, lessons are fun. I like reading and doing sums. And I like writing, too. And I do love hearing about other countries and other people."

"Well, you go then," said Willie, and he still didn't look at Fenella. She couldn't think why Willie was like this; it puzzled her.

"Look at me, Willie," she said suddenly. "Why don't you look at me when you speak, as you usually do?"

Willie glanced up at her and then looked away again. But he saw the disappointed face of the little girl and the tears shining in her eyes. He grunted.

Fenella stood for a moment longer, and then, as Willie still went on splashing the goose, she turned to go.

"Well, good-bye then," she said, still in a small voice. "I shan't enjoy lessons a bit without you."

She walked across the field to Presto's caravan. It was a black one, painted with silver and gold stars, moons and suns. At the door sat a big black cat, sunning itself. It always went into the ring with Presto and sat there solemnly, whilst he performed. Then it stalked out with him.

Fenella felt rather miserable. She didn't want to have lessons all alone with the solemn conjurer. She looked at the shut door of the caravan, and the cat sitting silently on the step. Should she knock? Would the cat mind her stepping over it? It looked as solemn as Presto himself!

She stood there for a moment, not quite knowing

what to do. Then she heard footsteps behind her, and a hand slipped through her arm.

"I'm coming, Fenny," said Willie's voice. "I hate to see you going off all alone! I'm coming, too!"

"Oh *Willie!*" said Fenella in delight, her face beaming. "Thank you! Now I feel quite different. Why have you changed your mind?"

Willie didn't tell her. His kind heart couldn't bear to see the little girl go off alone, looking so disappointed and sad. The boy grinned at her and knocked loudly at Presto's door, making the cat jump in fright and leap down the steps.

"Here we go!" said Willie. "And let's hope I please Presto, because I don't want to be turned into a cat like old Cinders there!"

"Come in!" said a quiet, low voice. They opened the door and went in. Now for lessons with the conjurer! Fenella wondered if they would enjoy them. She did hope so!

AT SCHOOL WITH THE CONJURER

PRESTO the conjurer was not dressed in his long, black, red-lined cloak now, nor was he wearing the tall pointed hat Fenella had seen him in the evening before. He sat at a table, dressed in a dark blue jersey and dark blue trousers, looking a little like a fisherman. His piercing eyes looked at both children, and Fenella felt sure he could see what she was thinking!

"Good morning," he said. "I am glad you have come. You are Fenella, are you not?"

His voice and way of speaking were not a bit like the voices of the other circus folk. He did not smile, but neither did he look cross. He just looked serious and solemn.

"Yes. I'm Fenella," said the little girl shyly. "It's kind of you to say you'll teach us, Mr. Presto."

"Can you read?" asked the conjurer. He pushed a book over to her, and flipped open a page. "Read me a little of this, if you can."

Fenella looked at it. It was very easy! She read out clearly from the page. "The cat saw a rat and it ran under a mat. The cat could not get the rat. The dog came up and——"

"Oh, that's too easy for you, I can see," said Presto. "Try this one."

He gave her another book. Fenella read from it at once. "The princess was lost in the wood. She looked all round, but the big dark trees shut out the sunlight, and she did not know which way to go. Suddenly——"

"Why, you can read as well as I can!" said Presto, sounding as if he was smiling. But he wasn't. He looked just as solemn as ever. "That is very good. You are the first circus child I have known who has been able to read without stumbling at your age."

"Well, I'm not really a circus child," explained Fenella. "Not till a few days ago, anyway. I lived with my aunt in a house and I went to school. I was top of my form sometimes, Mr. Presto."

"And now Willie," said Presto, handing Willie the first book he had given to Fenella. Willie took the book. Fenella saw that a wave of red was creeping over his face and even over his neck. What *could* be the matter?

Willie cleared his throat. "The cat," he began, "er, the cat saw a rat . . ."

"Wait," said Presto. "That is what Fenella read. I

have turned the page since then. Now the tale is about a dog."

"Oh," said Willie. He glued his eyes to the page. "The dog," he began, and stopped. Fenella peeped at where he was reading. "The dog ran," she helped him.

"The dog ran—to—the—er, er, to the, er—p——," stammered Willie. Fenella stared at him in surprise. Could it be that the wonderful, marvellous Willie Winkie the Whistler couldn't read even such little short words? Willie wouldn't look at Fenella.

"Oh, Willie! You *can't* read—and you said you could!" said Fenella.

"I thought I could," mumbled Willie. Presto took the book from his hands.

"You will soon be able to," he said. "If you come to me each day, Willie, you will learn much. You are a clever boy, as we all know. You will learn easily."

Willie cheered up a little. He took a quick look at Fenella to see if she was scornful of him. But she wasn't. She squeezed his arm.

"Oh, Willie, I shall be able to help you. Perhaps Aunt Lou would let me come to your caravan in the evenings with a book and we'll read it together. Oh, I'm glad I can do something better than you can, Willie, because now I shan't feel so small and silly. You see, everyone in this circus seems to be able to do something really wonderful, except me—even Cackles your goose. I can't help feeling glad that I can read better than you!"

Willie gave her his old cheerful grin. So long as Fenella didn't despise him for having so little learning, that was all right! Willie couldn't bear to be looked down on. The little girl smiled back.

"I'll soon read better than you can!" said Willie. "Shan't I, Presto?"

"We will see," said Presto. "Fenella, let me see how well you can write, whilst I help Willie a little with his reading."

Fenella settled down at the table with a pencil and an exercise book. She liked lessons. She meant to show Presto what beautiful writing she could do. She wrote carefully whilst Willie stammered through an easy page of reading.

Cinders, the big black cat, sauntered in and sat down on the table beside Fenella. The cat had the brightest green eyes that Fenella had ever seen. "Is he magic?" asked the little girl. "He looks as if he is."

"Then perhaps he is," said Presto. "We will draw a chalk ring round him, when we have finished lessons this morning—that is if you are a good girl—and we will say a few magic words, and see what happens."

Fenella felt excited. This was better than lessons at school. She had never had a magic cat sitting beside her there, waiting to have a chalk ring drawn round him. She bent to her writing again, listening to Willie's voice.

Presto was a good teacher. He was very patient, and he did not scold at all. Fenella looked at his solemn face, and she liked him. She liked the nice clean look he had, and his neat clothes, and she liked his quiet, well-spoken voice. He didn't seem like a circus performer at all.

Willie's writing was even worse than his reading. His arithmetic was queer. He could do any sum in his head, quickly and well—but he couldn't work out one that Presto set down on paper, not even the very easiest!

"Yes, my boy, you have a good and quick brain, and I tell you this—if you use it well and train it, you will go far," said Presto, in his serious voice. "But if you do not train it, it will not be of much use or pleasure to you. Only you can choose."

Willie was tired of lessons. He didn't like being cooped up in the caravan, when he could be out in the hills with dogs, or racing over the field with the horses. He looked at Presto, and felt that it would be a great bore to go on and on with lessons.

"Well, I'll try," he said at last. "But lots of the circus

76

folk get on quite well without much book-learning, Presto."

"They would get on even better with it," said Presto. "Now, Fenella, you have been a good girl, and you have written me out a fine page of writing—we will see if Cinders is a magic cat or not!"

Presto put Cinders down from the table, and then moved it across to the end of the caravan. He took up the rug below, showing a black-painted, highly-polished floor.

He made a curious noise with his tongue and Cinders strolled into the middle of the floor and sat down, curling his tail round him. He looked up at his master with his queer green eyes.

Presto drew a chalk circle round him. Then he chanted a queer string of words that Fenella thought must be magic. She listened half-fearfully. Willie watched with a smile on his face. He had seen many of Presto's wonderful tricks before.

The cat miaowed loudly three times. Then Presto spoke softly to him.

"Cinders, my cat, have you a present for the good little girl? Tell me, have you a present?"

"Miaow!" said Cinders loudly, and looked at Fenella.

"Well, come from the magic ring then, and let us see what you have got for Fenella," said Presto. The cat got up and walked out of the ring, its long black tail waving in the air. Where it had been sitting was a little white handkerchief, folded very small.

"There is your present, Fenella," said Presto. "Take it!"

"How did it get there?" asked Fenella, in wonder. "It wasn't there before Cinders went and sat down. It's magic!"

The picked up the little handkerchief and opened it. In one corner was embroidered a tiny black cat with green eyes, just like Cinders!

"Oh, it's lovely!" said Fenella, pleased. "Is it really

77

for me? Oh, thank you, Mr. Presto. Thank you, Cinders."

Willie grinned to hear Fenella thanking Cinders, who was now sitting with his back to them all, as if he was tired of being with them. Presto did not smile, but his eyes looked in a kindly way at Fenella.

"Come to-morrow," he said. "It is a pleasure to teach a good little girl like you."

The children left the caravan together. "His face doesn't smile at all, but his voice often does," said Fenella. "Oh, isn't it a fine hanky? The best I've ever had. Willie, didn't you like having lessons with Mr. Presto?"

"No, I didn't," said Willie. "My, I'm stiff with sitting so long! I'm going up in the hills with the dogs. Coming, Fenny?"

But Fenella couldn't because it was almost dinner-time, and she didn't want to get into trouble with Aunt Lou. "Isn't it your dinner-time, too?" she asked Willie.

"Oh, Mum doesn't mind what time we have our meals," said Willie. "Hallo, Cackles! Did you miss me? Maybe to-morrow I'll take you to lessons, too. Then you'll learn a lot!"

Fenella laughed and sped off to her aunt's caravan. She had enjoyed her morning, and she had the lovely little hanky to show her aunt that she really had pleased Presto. And this afternoon she would be able to work on some of the lovely circus clothes and get them ready for the night. Then she would be able to peep through those curtains again and watch the show. She would never get tired of that, never, whatever Willie said!

SOON a whole week had gone by. Fenella felt as if she had lived in the circus camp for months. She began to get used to the different life, and she liked it.

She helped her aunt with the caravan in the morning, and at ten o'clock she went with Willie to Presto's caravan. He took Cackles the goose on the second day, and as soon as Cinders saw her, he spat and hissed.

To his great surprise Cackles hissed back, even more loudly. Cinders arched his back and made his tail three times its usual size. The goose cackled loudly and Cinders leapt back in fright. He had never seen the goose so closely before, for Cinders was a home-cat and hardly ever left the caravan.

Then Cackles put her head neatly under her wing, meaning to settle down and go to sleep, whilst Willie did whatever he wanted to do in this strange caravan. Cinders was amazed to see the goose's head disappear.

"Aha! The goose can also do magic, Cinders," said Presto, in what Fenella called his "smiling voice." "Willie, if you want your goose to come to lessons, she must wait outside for you. I cannot have Cinders spitting and hissing like damp wood on a fire all the time! "

So Cackles had to wait outside. She squatted down on the top step in the sun, much to Cinders' annoyance, for that was his own favourite place. But nothing would shift the big, heavy goose once she had taken up her place. Cinders did not like the look of that quick beak, either!

In the afternoons Fenella settled down with her aunt to do the circus mending. There always seemed plenty to do. Aunt Lou grumbled because she said the circus folk were so careless with their clothes.

"If they had to sew up their holes themselves, and stitch back the ripped frills, they'd be more careful," she said, threading her needle. "And look at this skirt of Mrs. Connie's. I believe she tears it on purpose! This is the third day she's sent it in for mending."

"I'll do it, Aunt Lou," said Fenella, knowing that her aunt would go on grumbling all the time, if she had to spend an hour or two on Mrs. Connie's clothes. The monkey woman had not dared to send in any of her monkeys' clothes since her quarrel with Aunt Lou. One or two of them were beginning to look rather ragged, but Fenella didn't like to offer to mend them herself. She was afraid of making another upset between the two.

At tea-time they stopped work and Fenella watched the circus folk getting ready as usual for their evening show. There was always such a bustle then, and the little girl was surprised to see how often the circus folk lost or forgot something they needed for the ring that night.

"Where's my balancing stick?" Mr. Wriggle would moan. "I put it down somewhere. I can't walk the tight-rope without it. Anybody seen it?"

"Oh—that must have been what Grin or Bearit was carrying!" Fenella would say. "I wondered what it was. Oh dear, Mr. Wriggle, I hope those chimps haven't broken it!"

"They've hidden it in Mr. Holla's caravan, I expect," Mr. Wriggle would say. "That's where they always hide their treasures. Thanks, Fenella. I say—you wouldn't like to see me tread on my head, would you?"

"Oh no, thank you, Mr. Wriggle," Fenella would say. "I should hate it. Please don't keep asking me that."

But Wriggle always did ask her. She had never seen him tread on his head yet, and she hoped she never would. She thought he was very, very clever the way he wriggled his rubbery body into all sorts of queer positions, but she didn't like it. He was a most remarkable acrobat, and great friends with everyone.

Wriggle wasn't the only one who was always losing things. Mrs. Connie lost things regularly, and so did Aggie, Willie's mother. Fenella got quite good at finding what was lost, and everyone agreed that the little girl was very useful. Aunt Lou began to feel rather proud of her.

She didn't say so, though. She was still as sharp-tongued as ever, and if Fenella sewed a wrong button on, or made a frill a little crooked, she would fly out at her in a great rage. Uncle Ursie used to look quite troubled when he heard Aunt Lou scolding the little girl.

"Now, you turn that tongue of yours on me instead," he would say. "I don't mind it, Lou. I'm used to it. All you say runs off my back like water off Cackles' feathers. But Fenella isn't used to it. She's a good little thing and you shouldn't scold her like that."

"It's good for children to get a good scolding now and again," Aunt Lou would say. "And don't you interfere with me, Ursie, or you'll be sorry!"

On Saturdays two shows were given, one in the afternoon, and one in the evening. So there were no lessons that day, and any sewing and mending that had to be done was done in the mornings. The circus folk were tired on Saturday night. Tempers were sometimes short then. Fenella heard Micko and Tricks, two of the clowns, quarrelling in loud voices, and she was alarmed.

"I'll leave!" shouted Micko. "I won't work with you again, Tricks! Getting all the laughs for yourself, and behaving as if you hadn't got a partner. I'll go off to Nicky's show, and leave you by yourself!"

"Oh dear! Will he really do that?" Fenella asked Uncle Ursie. "Micko's so fond of Tricks. They've been together for years, haven't they?"

"They'll have made it up by to-morrow night," said Uncle Ursie, comfortingly. "There's plenty of hot tempers in a circus like this, but they simmer down usually. If they don't, Mr. Crack comes along, and he soon settles things, I can tell you! "

And sure enough, by the next night, after a quiet, peaceful Sunday, with church bells ringing from the villiages around, Micko and Tricks were as good friends as ever, and Fenella, to her joy, saw them walking round the camp, arm in arm as usual. She really couldn't bear anyone to quarrel.

"I shall never quarrel with you, Willie," she said to him. "And you'll never quarrel with me, will you?"

"I shouldn't think so," said Willie. "But you never know! Things blow up suddenly, you know."

"Well—it takes two to make a quarrel—and you can quarrel all you like with me, but I shan't quarrel back! " said Fenella. "Willie, when do we move on? It will be fun to feel our caravan moving along on its wheels. I've never been in one that went along the road."

"We'll be on the road in a week's time," said Willie. "And I believe we're going to a seaside place, Fenella. You'll like that. We can take the dogs for their run on the sands each day—or up on to the cliffs. And maybe we'll bathe. I can't swim though. Can you?"

"Yes," said Fenella, happy to think that here was one more thing she could do that Willie couldn't. "I'll teach you. It's easy. Cackles can swim with us! "

The days flew past. Nothing much happened those last few days except that Grin disgraced himself by escaping from the camp, going to a nearby house, and picking every single flower in the garden there. He came back delighted with himself, carrying a most enormous bunch of all kinds of flowers.

Mr. Crack was not pleased. He roared at poor Mr. Holla. "Look after your chimps better than that! Are we to have the police here, because of them? You will pay to the lady of that house whatever she asks you for the flowers."

Grin was sternly punished. His cap was taken away,

and he hated that, for he was always very proud of wearing a cap. He was made to stay in his cage the whole of one day, instead of going about the camp with Willie or Mr. Holla or anyone who would take him. Everyone was forbidden to speak to him for that day.

Fenella was very sorry for him. She felt sure Grin hadn't meant to be naughty. He had seen the flowers and liked them, so he had picked them. But Grin did know better than that! He had done it out of mischief, and Mr. Holla knew he must punish him.

The last show in that district was a great success. Everyone did better than usual. Mr. Groggy gave away twice as many balloons. Mrs. Connie's monkeys threw bars of chocolate to the cheering children on the benches. Millie bit hers in half before she threw it, and kept a bit for herself. Mrs. Connie found it stuffed into Millie's little hat that night!

Dicky, Domo and Dolly hit balls out to the audience, and Mr. Tiny yelled that any boy or girl who caught one could keep it. Altogether it was an exciting and glorious evening, and Mr. Crack was in such a good temper that he didn't stop smiling once the whole evening. In fact, Presto was the only one who neither smiled nor laughed, but Fenella thought that even he had a twinkle in his eye.

"Why don't you smile?" she asked him, when he came to stand by her, to listen to the cheering that followed the elephants' fine performance. "You never smile, Mr. Presto. *Can't* you?"

Presto said nothing. Willie pulled at Fenella's sleeve. "Don't ask him that," he whispered. "Something dreadful once happened to him, and he vowed he would never smile again. So he never will!"

Fenella felt sorry she had said anything. She crept away, looking back at the tall, solemn figure in the great black cloak and pointed hat. There were times when Fenella really did think Preston was an enchanter out of

Fairyland. He looked so very striking with his deep dark eyes and his jet-black hair.

The circus had done very well indeed in those two weeks. Mr. Crack made a most generous share-out, and everyone received a good amount of money. Even Aunt Lou was pleased, and she gave Fenella a shilling for herself.

"Oh, thank you!" said Fenella. And then Uncle Ursie gave her two shillings! Fenella felt that she was rich. She would buy ice creams for herself and Willie. And did Cackles like them, too? She knew Grin and Bearit did, and as for little Bobbo, he would lick a dozen up if he could.

"To-morrow we pack up and go off," said Uncle Ursie to Fenella. "That's a job, I can tell you! The animals don't like it, either. They'll make a fine old noise. You can take charge of Bobbo, if you like. He's so fond of you now he'll do anything for you, and you will be able to keep him quiet and happy."

"Oh, I will," promised Fenella happily. She looked forward to the move It might be a tiresome job for the circus folk—but it would be all new to Fenella.

"Our caravan will roll away on its wheels," she told Rosebud, her doll, in bed that night. "How will you like that? A house that moves by itself, and goes for miles and miles. Won't it be exciting!"

THE CIRCUS GOES ON THE ROAD

THE next day the circus folk were busier than Fenella had yet seen them. The big top, the great circus tent, had to be taken down. All the benches had to be stored neatly on big lorries. The various circus properties such as steel posts for the tight-rope wire, the tennis net the elephants used for their game, odd tables and chairs, had to be packed into another lorry.

The camp was due to set off at a certain time. All the vans, carts, cars and lorries were to start one after another. The lorries would go on in front, Mr. Crack's lovely car-drawn caravan would follow, and then all the horse-drawn caravans and carts.

"What about the elephants?" asked Fenella, watching Uncle Ursie sliding shut the side of the bears' cage. "Do they go in a travelling cage, too? I haven't seen one big enough for them."

"Oh, no. They walk," said Uncle Ursie. "They are rather slow, so they'll start last, and catch us up at night."

Grin and Bearit were shut up in Mr. Holla's caravan. The door was locked, and the windows were fastened, so that the chimps were safe. Fenella saw their hairy faces peeping out of the window, looking rather dismal.

The monkeys were all in their own little caravan. The dogs were in their travelling cage, restless and rather bad-tempered at being shut up, after their long time of freedom. The lovely circus horses were to be ridden in a long string by Fric, Frac and Malvina.

"Who's going to drive Mr. Crack's lovely golden carriage?" asked Fenella. "We're going to take that too, aren't we?"

"Of course!" said Uncle Ursie. "Maybe Willie will drive it. He did last time. Malvina says it bores her to do a thing like that when she can take the string of horses along with Fric and Frac!"

"Oh—is Willie *really* going to drive the golden carriage?" cried Fenella. "Uncle Ursie, do you think he would let me drive it with him?"

"I didn't know you *could* drive!" said Uncle Ursie. He was putting the old brown horse that belonged to him and Aunt Lou, into the shafts of their red caravan. "Hey, get up there. Anyone would think you'd never been between shafts before, Dobbin!"

"I *can't* drive," said Fenella. "I really meant—would Willie let me sit with him? Oh, I would so love that! You don't suppose I could sit in that carriage, do you?"

"I don't see why not," said Uncle Ursie. "Why, would it make you feel very grand, Fenny?"

"Oh yes—I'd feel like a princess!" cried Fenella. Then her face fell. "But do you think Aunt Lou would mind, Uncle Ursie? She has been rather cross to-day."

"Oh, nobody likes moving day," said Uncle Ursie. "There you are, Dobbin, you're in at last. Now don't you go galloping off till I'm ready!"

Fenella smiled. Dobbin didn't look as if he could gallop two steps! He was the fattest barrel of a horse Fenella had ever seen. She liked him. He had big brown eyes, and he nuzzled into her shoulder when she went near. Fenella was often very surprised at herself nowadays. She did things she would never never have dreamt of doing three weeks before. Why, she would never go within yards of a horse before she came to the circus! Now she spoke to every one of them, and had learnt to caress them in the same affectionate way as all the circus folk.

Fenella sat on the steps of her caravan and watched and busy scene in the field. The lorries were moving off through the gate, heavily laden, each covered up in tarpaulin sheets to keep everything safe and dry. Then went Mr. Carl Crack's car, driven by himself, his fine caravan bumping heavily over the ruts in the field.

He raised his top-hat as he went out of the gate. "See you later!" he roared to everyone, and they waved back. Then down the narrow lane went his caravan, drawn by the powerful car.

Dicky, Dolly and Domo, the three elephants, were waiting patiently under the tree for the time to come when they could walk out of the gate, too. Domo trumpeted loudly. Mr. Tiny patted him on the trunk.

"Now don't be so impatient. You know we go last of all. We'll be there in good time."

Then the brightly-coloured caravans began to move out of the field gate, one by one, drawn by the caravan horses—quite different creatures from the proud, shining circus horses. Dobbin and Clover, Daisy and Brownie, Star and Grumps, all the ordinary horses, now came into their own, and hauled along the caravans, walking slowly and peacefully.

"When do the circus horses go?" asked Fenella, watching everything, and waiting impatiently for her caravan's turn to come.

"They're going a different way, over the commons and through the woods," said Uncle Ursie. "Better for them than hard roads. There they go now. Malvina's on the leading horse. What that girl can't do with horses isn't worth doing! They say she was put on a horse before she was two months old!"

Malvina, looking as spruce and smart as ever, sat lightly on the beautiful leading horse. She was one of the few circus folk who looked as lovely out of the ring as in it. She and Fric and Frac spent most of the time with their beloved horses, and Fenella had had hardly a word with them at all. They were always so busy.

More caravans passed out of the gate. There went the two caravans belonging to Mrs. Connie. Fenella

87

could hear all the monkeys chattering together excitedly in one of them. Mrs. Connie, looking more like a monkey than ever, drove the first caravan. Micko drove the monkeys' van, with Tricks whistling beside him.

Mr. Groggy's van went Presto's striking black one slid out of the gate, too, drawn by a jet-black horse. Presto drove the caravan himself, looking as solemn as ever, and beside him, solemn and serious, too, sat Cinders the black cat.

"I'm sure Cinders is a witch-cat," thought Fenella, watching. "Oh, there go the chimps. Poor Grin and Bearit, they don't like being locked up."

Then came Fenella's turn. The travelling cage of the bears was driven by Uncle Ursie, and the red caravan by Aunt Lou. A little white pony pulled the bears' van, trotting quickly along, tossing its white mane.

"He used to belong to Malvina's string of snow-white ponies," said Uncle Ursie. "But he's too old now for the ring. So I bought him from Malvina for the bears' van. He's glad to stay with the circus. He'd be very lonely without all the people he knows."

Fenella climbed into the red caravan. She wanted to feel the very first movement it made. Aunt Lou clicked to Dobbin. He took a step forward and pulled the cart. Fenella felt it moving—then it ran bumpily along on its four wheels. They were off!

"Our house is rumbling away on its journey!" said Fenella to herself in delight. "It feels lovely. Bumpity-bump, shakity-shake, there it goes over the field where we have stayed so long. Oh, I do like it better than a house with its roots in the ground. It's fun to have a house that moves! Go on, Dobbin, go on!"

They passed the little golden carriage into which Willie was now putting the six snow-white ponies. Fenella yelled to him as she passed.

"Willie, we're going! Do, do catch us up. And Willie, could I sit with you and Cackles sometime, please?"

"Goodness, child, don't yell in my ear like that," said

Aunt Lou. Fenella dropped off the caravan and ran to Willie.

"Willie, did you hear me? Can I come with you part of the time?"

"Course you can," said Willie. "There'll be room on the driving seat for both you and Cackles, too. And maybe you'd like to ride in the golden carriage whenever we pass through a town or village. That will make everyone stare!"

"Oh, Willie, could I?" said Fenella in delight. "I did just wonder if I could. Do keep close behind us if you can, for I'm sure Aunt Lou won't let me out of her sight if she can help it."

"Fenella! FENELLA!" yelled Uncle Ursie's deep voice. "Come along. We're waiting."

"Coming!" called Fenella, and raced across the field to the gate. She clambered up beside Uncle Ursie, in front of the bears' van, for she saw that Aunt Lou had rather an impatient look on her face, and she did not want to drive with her.

Off they went. Out of the gate and down the lane, right to the bottom of the hill and up another one. The wind blew freshly, and the sun shone down warmly. Buttercup fields spread golden on every side. Fenella felt very happy indeed.

Aunt Lou called her. "Fenella! I haven't had time to tidy up the caravan this morning. You go in and do it, there's a good girl."

Fenella skipped down from beside Uncle Ursie and ran a few steps in front. She climbed up into the red caravan, and began to tidy it. It was queer to stand in it whilst it rumbled and jolted about, but it was fun. Fenella noticed that Aunt Lou had put away everything that might fall and break.

"I've done it, Aunt Lou," she said, and climbed up beside her aunt. "Isn't this lovely? I do like going on a journey like this, don't you?"

"Well, I've done it so many times that I don't really
89

notice it," said Aunt Lou. But all the same she seemed to like the peaceful jogtrot of the horse, and looked round at the buttercup fields with pleasure.

"My little girl used to like those," she said, with a nod of her head. Fenella wanted to ask her about her little girl, but she didn't like to. So she said nothing. Dobbin jogged on and on, and after some time Fenella began to feel hungry. Suddenly her aunt put the reins into her hands.

"You drive now, Fenella," she said. "I'll go and get something for us to eat."

"Oh, Aunt Lou! I can't drive Dobbin!" cried Fenella in fright. But Aunt Lou had jumped down and was going to the door of the caravan. Fenella *had* to drive! She stared ahead in fright, clutching the reins.

But Dobbin didn't need any driving. He knew that all he had to do was to follow the van in front, and to go at the same slow pace. It didn't matter to him whether Aunt Lou held the reins, or Fenny. In fact it didn't really matter whether *anyone* held the reins. Dobbin would go on for miles all by himself!

So in a few minutes Fenella got over her fright and began to enjoy herself. She was driving a caravan! Whatever would her Aunt Janet say if she saw her—and all the children she had once known at school, too!

"I feel important!" said Fenella to herself. "I really do. I belong to a circus. I'm driving a real live horse in a caravan! I wish Rosebud was beside me. Aunt Lou! *Please* could I have Rosebud? Do let me!"

And for once in a way Aunt Lou smiled and gave Rosebud to Fenella through one of the little front windows. There they sat, side by side, Fenella and Rosebud, enjoying themselves immensely. What a lovely journey!

FENELLA IN TROUBLE

PRESENTLY a shout came from the front of the long line of horses and caravans. It was passed along from one to another.

"We're stopping on the common! We're stopping on the common!"

When the procession came to the big open common, the caravans were all drawn up to the side. The horses were taken out for a rest and a feed, and were set free. They were all too well-trained to wander away, but kept near the circus folk, cropping the grass peacefully.

May trees were still out, and the scent of them filled the air as Fenella sat down on the dry, wiry grass with Willie, Cackles, Aunt Aggie, Aunt Lou and Uncle Ursie. There were sardine sandwiches, egg sandwiches, sausage rolls and two kinds of cake. There was a bag of oranges, too, so the two children had a good feast.

Cackles pulled at the grass around, but did not seem to like it very much. She came to share Willie's sandwiches. Willie offered her a lettuce and she took it greedily, tearing it to bits with her strong yellow beak.

"She loves lettuce," said Willie to Fenella.

"Does she like ice cream?" asked Fenella, remembering the three shillings she had.

"No," said Willie. "Good thing, too. She'd gobble down about a dozen if she did!"

"Bobbo likes them," said Fenella. "Uncle Ursie said so. I'm going to buy ice creams for us, Willie, next time I see an ice cream man!"

They lazed on the sunny grass, enjoying their rest. Some of the horses lay down. The animals in the caravans cried to be let out. They could never understand why they had to be shut up during the journeys from place to place.

Fenella thought of Bobbo. She was sure she could hear him whimpering. "Uncle Ursie! Please, please do go and get Bobbo," she begged. "I'm sure he's unhappy. I want to give him an ice cream, and I expect an ice cream man will come along soon."

"Too lazy to move!" said Uncle Ursie, sleepily. He was lying on his back on the grass, his eyes shut. Aunt Lou was talking to Willie's mother. Fenella didn't like to bother Uncle Ursie any more about Bobbo. What a pity! She heard the bell of an ice cream man, and jumped up "Six sixpenny ice creams, please," she said, and the man took six from his ice-cold barrel.

Fenella gave one to Willie. He was thrilled. "Just what I wanted," he said. "Thanks, Fenny."

"One for you, Aunt Aggie," said Fenella, "and one for you, Aunt Lou."

The two women looked up, surprised. "Well, if that isn't generous of you, Fenella!" said Aunt Aggie. "Thank you. Spending your money on us like that! I declare that's just like your own little Carol used to do, Lou. Soon as she had a penny, off she'd go and spend it on someone."

"Yes," said Aunt Lou, and she looked pleased, too. "That's nice of you, Fenella. But remember that you must save money as well as spend it!"

"Oh yes, Aunt," said Fenella hastily, hoping that Aunt Lou wouldn't ask her how much money she had left out of her three shillings. She would have to say none at all!

"Uncle Ursie! Here's an ice cream for you," said Fenella, and pommelled him. "Do wake up, or it will be melted. And Uncle Ursie, please can I go and give this one to Bobbo? I bought it for him."

"Good gracious! One for Bobbo!" said Uncle Ursie, opening his eyes. "Well, here's the key of the cage. Go and give the ice cream to him."

Fenella took the key and went back to where the bears' caravan was drawn up to the side of the road. She slid the key into the lock and turned it. She opened the door and went in. Bobbo was in a corner, rolled up in a ball, whimpering to himself. Fenella picked him up.

"Dear little bear!" she said. "I've got an ice cream for you Come and have it!"

She took him out of the caravan, and went over to Willie. Then she fed Bobbo with the ice cream and he made little grunting noises of delight. Fenella and Willie ate their ice creams, too, whilst Cackles looked on. Bobbo made himself into a mess, but licked it all off with his red tongue.

Nobody noticed that Fenella had left the door of the bears' van open. Nobody saw Clump come to the opening and look out. Nobody knew that he had crept out from the van and gone into the bushes. He was so very, very quiet!

But suddenly, from over the common, came a scream. Then another and another. Everyone sat up in fright. What was the matter?

"Help! Help!" came the voice, and then it screamed again. "Save us, save us!"

Uncle Ursie, Willie, Micko and Tricks raced over the common to where the voice came from. Fenella could still hear it. "Oh, help, help, help!"

In a little hollow were two ladies having a picnic. They had just laid themselves down to have a little sleep, when they heard the crackling of twigs.

When they looked up, what did they see but a big, brown bear looking down at them! No wonder they screamed. A bear! A bear on the common they walked over each day! Could it be true?

Clump looked at the two scared women. When they screamed, he was frightened and growled. That scared them all the more. They clutched one another in fright.

Clump certainly startled them

Clump decided to try and please these noisy women. So he solemny turned head-over-heels three times and then sat and looked at them, holding a paw as if to say: "There you are! I did it for you! Do be friends!"

It was just then that Uncle Ursie and the others came into the little hollow. They saw Clump there and the two frightened women. Uncle Ursie spoke sternly to Clump.

"Clump! How dare you wander off like this? Come here!"

Clump came obediently to Uncle Ursie. He pushed his head against him, trying to make his master understand that he hadn't meant to do any harm. Uncle Ursie spoke calmly to the two women.

"Don't be afraid. He is quite harmless. May I ask you to accept two tickets for our circus? Then you will see the bear perform."

"It ought to be reported to the police," said one of the women angrily.

"You would only get the poor bear into trouble," said Uncle Ursie. "I'm very sorry, Madam. Pray do take the tickets to make up for your fright. Perhaps you have children who would like to use them, if you don't want to."

His politeness had a very good effect on the two women. They smiled and took the tickets. "Well, we did have a fright!" said one to the other. "Quite an adventure!"

Uncle Ursie took Clump quickly back to the caravan. He looked cross. "What was all the screaming about?" asked Aunt Lou.

"Clump got out and wandered loose," said Uncle Ursie. He didn't say anything about the unlocked door. But Fenella knew at once that it was her fault. She went very red indeed. She got up with Bobbo in her arms and went over to Uncle Ursie.

"Uncle! It was my fault that Clump got out. How *could* I have been so careless as to leave the door open!

Oh, Uncle, please forgive me. I won't do it again."

"You might have got poor Clump into serious trouble," said Uncle Ursie severely, but he didn't look quite so cross. "If you have anything to do with animals in a circus you must be very careful about open doors. I shouldn't have given you the key. Now, give me Bobbo. He must go back again into the van."

When Aunt Lou knew what had happened she scolded Fenella, too. The little girl was very much upset, and cried. Willie was sorry for her.

"Cheer up," he said. "We all do silly things sometimes. You come along now and get into the golden carriage! That will cheer you up!"

"Oh *can* I, Willie?" said Fenella, drying her eyes and smiling a watery smile. "I'd love that. I'll bring Rosebud, too."

"We're passing through two or three villages soon," said Willie, taking her to where the carriage was. He put the little white ponies in, and then climbed up to the driver's seat. "Now, you get in, Fenella, and we'll drive off before your aunt can stop us!"

Fenella got into the little golden carriage, and sat down. She put Rosebud beside her. Cackles flew up by Willie. The boy clicked, and the ponies trotted off, drawing the golden carriage behind them.

Fenella sat in it like a little princess, feeling very grand indeed. The carriage passed Uncle Ursie and Aunt Lou. They stared in surprise. Aunt Lou was just about to shout to Fenella to come back, when Uncle Ursie put his hand on her arm.

"Let her be," he said. "She's had a good scolding this afternoon. But she was a generous girl with her ice creams for everybody, wasn't she—so let her have her little treat."

And Aunt Lou closed her mouth again and did not call to Fenella after all. Away went the little girl in the carriage, full of delight. When they came to a village all the children there came out to see the circus procession—

96

and how they stared to see Fenella in the golden carriage!

"Look at her! She's like Cinderella! " shouted a boy. "Cinderella had a golden carriage, didn't she? My, isn't she grand! "

"Hey, look at the goose! " yelled another child. "Is it a live one?"

"Cackle, cackle, cackle! " said the goose, and everyone knew she was alive all right!

What fun it was riding in the golden carriage, or sitting squashed in between Willie and Cackles on the driving seat! Fenella thought she had never had such a happy day before.

She was very tired when the procession halted for the night. Again they came to a common, and drew up all the vans and carts there, letting the horses loose.

Night came down, and the stars shone out. On the common camp-fires began to gleam as the circus folk lighted them to cook a meal. Soon the smell of frying bacon mingled with the smell of may. Fenella cuddled against her Uncle Ursie, almost too tired to eat anything, but enjoying the starry night, and the queerness of camping out in a strange place she didn't know.

She fell asleep leaning against her uncle. He lifted her up, and her doll, too. "I'll just pop her into her bunk as she is," he said to Aunt Lou. "She's tired out! "

Then, after a time, the camp-fires died down, and one by one the circus folk went into their caravans to sleep, calling good-night to one another. Their animals slept, too.

"Good night," said Willie to Cackles. "Sleep well! Happy dreams, Cackles—and don't wake me too early to-morrow! "

E

WHEN Fenella woke up the next morning, the first thing she heard was the trumpeting of the three elephants. She sat up in her bunk and looked out of the little window above her head. She saw Mr. Holla on the common nearby with Grin and Bearit, and behind him were Mr. Tiny and the elephants.

"Oh, the elephants caught us up all right then," thought Fenella, pleased. "They hadn't arrived when I fell asleep last night. I don't even remember going to bed."

She was up and about very quickly. Willie took her to the nearest stream, and she washed herself in the clear, cool water.

"We always have to camp near water," Willie told her, "because of the animals. They want plenty to drink. Look at Fric and Frac and Malvina setting off already. They joined us in the night, too—did you hear them? Now they are going off a different way again, over those green hills you can see over there. They probably won't touch a road at all! I went with them once and helped with the horses when Fric strained his side. We had a fine time."

Once more the long line of caravans moved off, when the circus folk had had their breakfast. It was a lovely day again. Fenella sat beside Uncle Ursie, chattering happily. He listened to her, pleased.

"You're good company, little Fenny," he said. "Your tongue is never still now, but I like to hear you talking away. And my, how brown you're getting! Quite one of us now, you look."

Fenella was indeed getting brown. All the circus folk were as brown as berries, for most of their life was passed out of doors.

"I haven't got as many freckles as Willie, though!" said Fenella. "His face is covered with them. He's got two dimples, like Aunt Aggie's, that go in and out. Did you know, Uncle Ursie?"

"Well, I can't say I ever noticed that," said Uncle Ursie, smiling. He clicked to the little white pony, and it trotted a little faster to catch up with Aunt Lou's caravan. "Let me take the reins," said Fenella. "I'd like to. I can drive now, Uncle Ursie."

"Well, you get Willie to let you drive Malvina's six ponies!" said Uncle Ursie. "They need a bit more driving than old Snowy here."

"Oh no! One horse is quite enough for me," said Fenella. Uncle Ursie handed her the reins, and she took them proudly. "See, Rosebud," she said to her doll, who was sitting beside her as usual. "See how well I drive!"

"Rosebud could drive Snowy just as well as you!" said Uncle Ursie, teasingly. "Here, you look!"

He took the reins from Fenella and twisted them round Rosebud's small arms. Snowy trotted along as if he hadn't noticed anything at all!

"Rosebud's clever, isn't she?" said Uncle Ursie, laughing at Fenella's face. He gave the reins back to the little girl. Snowy trotted on and on. In front stretched the line of caravans, and behind, too. Sometimes, when they climbed a hill, Fenella could see the whole lot, one behind the other.

"Shall we get there to-night, wherever we're going?" asked Fenella. "I wouldn't mind if it took us weeks, Uncle Ursie. I like this."

"Oh, we'll be there this afternoon, I expect," said her uncle. "Clump and Bobbo will be glad. They wouldn't like to go on the road for long. They hate being shut up. So do all the animals."

"Oh, yes. I forgot about them," said Fenella. She peered back through the small window that looked into the bears' van. "Poor Bobbo. He can't understand it. He keeps curled up in a ball, and whimpers. Clump's walking up and down and growling, Uncle."

The caravans stopped at dinner-time again for a meal,

but not for long. Then on they went, and suddenly, from the top of a hill, Fenella saw something blue that spread out flat before her, about a mile away. She gave a cry.

"Oh, the sea! Willie, Willie, look, can you see the blue water? It's the sea!"

She went to sit beside Willie and Cackles. "Soon be there now," said Willie, and he pointed to where a big, sloping field lay on a cliff overlooking the sea. "That's where we're camping. A bit windy, but that will be nice this hot weather. There'll be a little path down the cliff to the sea, I expect. What fun the dogs will have on the sands!"

"Bobbo will like it, too," said Fenella. "So shall I!"

By tea-time the circus caravans were up on the high field. The wind blew strongly. "Have to see that the big top is put up very carefully," said Uncle Ursie to Willie. "A bit more of a wind and the tent would fly over into the sea!"

Mr. Carl Crack's caravan was already in the field, and so were the big lorries laden with the circus properties. As the caravans streamed into the gateway of the field, there came the sound of horses' hooves, and Fenella gave a shout.

"Hurrah! Here are the horses, too! Now we only want the three elephants, and we'll all be together again."

Aunt Lou had done a bit of shopping at the last town they had come through. Her larder was now well-stocked, and she had bought more cottons and buttons, and some gay cloth. She showed the cloth to Fenella.

"This is for Mr. Holla. He wants a new suit for the ring. You can help me to make it."

"Oh, I should like to," said Fenella. "And how I should like to make a suit for little Bobbo, too, Aunt Lou. He's so sweet and funny—really like a little bear-clown. I'd like to make him a tiny clown suit, and a pointed hat like Groggy's, with black bobbles on it."

The circus folk began to settle down in their new camp. The caravans were pulled together to shelter each other from the strong wind. The field sloped down almost to sea-level at one corner, and here there ran a bubbling brook, which joined the sea, running over the sand. Mr. Holla took his elephants down to it as soon as they arrived. They were hot and dusty, and they enjoyed squirting themselves with the cool, clear water.

Grin and Bearit went too near them, and were squirted, too. But they liked that, and danced round the great elephants, getting wetter and wetter till Mr. Holla yelled to them to come away.

By the time that night came, the camp was quite settled in. The big top was not yet up, nor were the lorries unpacked. They would have to wait till the next day. It was enough that all the horses had been settled in, fed and watered, that the animals were now happy and comfortable, and the circus folk at peace after their two days' journey.

The smell of cooking arose, as Aunt Aggie, Mr. Tiny, Malvina, Aunt Lou and Mr. Groggy all began to fry bacon, sausages and tomatoes at the same time, on fires built cleverly of twigs, criss-crossed over one another. Fenella sniffed with pleasure.

"Oh, how lovely! And are those tinned pears and cream for us, Aunt Lou? You do get nice meals."

"Ah, you wait till we get a rainy week or two, and nobody comes to our shows, so that money is short!" said Aunt Lou. "Then you won't get nice meals! You'll have to make do with bread and margarine then. But whilst we've got the money we feed well."

"Do the animals have to go short of food, too, when money doesn't come in?" asked Fenella, thinking that it would be dreadful if Bobbo went hungry.

"Good gracious no, child! Whoever goes hungry the animals don't. You may be sure of that. Your uncle would rather starve than see Clump or Bobbo hungry. And Willie would go without food for days to feed Cackles and those dogs."

"And I'd go without this nice supper if I thought Bobbo was hungry," said Fenella, seriously. Uncle

Ursie heard her, and was touched. He gave Fenella a hug.

"Why, if you're not a proper little circus kid already, Fenny! That's the way to talk! Did you hear that, Lou? That's the kind of thing our Carol would have said, isn't it now?"

Aunt Lou said nothing to that, but pursed up her lips a little. Fenella couldn't tell if she was angry or sad. But she wasn't angry, it was clear, because she gave Fenella the kind of sausage she liked best of all, rather burnt, and burst a little at one side.

"Oh, thank you, Aunt Lou," said Fenella. "That's how I like sausages best! I *am* hungry! I was never so hungry in my life before as I have been since I've come to live with you."

"You'll grow as fat as Bobbo!" said Aunt Lou, in an unexpectedly pleasant voice. "Never mind if you do. You could do with a bit more fat on you. Your legs are too skinny."

Fenella went to find Willie after she had had her supper and helped to do the washing-up. Willie was putting the dogs back into their big travelling cage, after having taken them for a short run. Cackles was nearby as usual, hissing if any dog came too near.

"I'll get Bobbo for a minute!" said Fenella and ran to ask Uncle Ursie if she could have him. He nodded. "But no leaving the door open, now, Fenny!"

Fenella took Bobbo over to Willie and Cackles. The goose was quite used to the fat little bear now, and liked him. Bobbo went up to her, stood up on his hind legs and waved a clumsy paw.

"Oh, look! Bobbo is standing up all by himself!" said Fenella, pleased. "And he's waving a paw at Cackles. Isn't he funny? Oh—down he goes with a bump. He always looks so *very* astonished when he sits down suddenly like that, doesn't he, Willie?"

"Cackle, cackle," said Cackles, and pulled gently at one of Bobbo's hind paws with her beak.

"She's telling him to get up!" said Fenella. They

played with the bear and the goose till it got too dark to see. Then Fenella heard her aunt calling and ran off with Bobbo in her arms.

"I shall like to go to bed to-night, hearing the sound of the sea all the time," she said to Aunt Lou. "It's a lovely noise. And I like this wind, too, too. It's got a nice seaweedy smell. Can I go and paddle to-morrow, Aunt Lou?"

"If you do your lessons, and help me nicely with the sewing," said Aunt Lou. "Brush your hair well to-night. It's all tangled with the wind."

Soon Fenella was ready to climb into her bunk. She stood on the steps of the caravan in her nightie. The wind blew round her legs and she liked it. "Good night, Uncle Ursie! Good night, Aunt Lou! Won't it be nice to wake up and see the blue sea to-morrow? Good night!"

WILLIE AND FENELLA

FENELLA awoke to the sound of the sea the next day. She lay in her bunk and listened to it. She had only once before been to the seaside, and she felt very happy to think that she was going to be near it for some time.

"Perhaps Bobbo will like to paddle and bathe with me," she thought. "And I'm sure Grin and Bearit will. We shall have a lovely time!"

After breakfast she asked her aunt if she was to go to Presto for her usual lessons. "Of course," said Aunt Lou. "It's nearly ten o'clock. Take the book he gave you to write in and go."

"Can I take Bobbo, too?" asked Fenella. "Willie always takes Cackles."

"Certainly not," said her aunt. "Go along now. Find Willie."

Willie was just about to let the dogs out and take them

on the seashore. "Willie! Aren't you going to lessons?" cried Fenella, running up.

"What! The first day we're here?" said Willie. "Presto won't expect us."

"Oh, yes, I do," said the conjurer's voice, and Presto walked round the caravan. "I might give Fenella here a holiday, Willie, but not you! You have a lot to learn—more than Fenella has."

Willie didn't like that. He put on a sulky look that Fenella had only seen once or twice before.

"I can't come to-day. I've got to take the dogs out."

"You can do that when you have finished with me," said Presto, his voice going rather cold and stern. "I do not arrange to give up my time for nothing, Willie. You will come now."

Fenella stared anxiously at Willie. He still looked sulky. But he, too, had heard that warning note in Presto's voice. He slammed the door of the dogs' cage shut, almost nipping Bouncer's nose.

He followed Fenella to Presto's black caravan, still looking sulky. On the way they met Mr. Crack, striding over the field to look at the horses. He nodded to Presto.

"Got your two pupils, Presto? That's good! I hope they are getting on well. They are lucky to get this schooling from you!"

Willie scowled. Mr. Crack raised his shaggy eyebrows. "Well, Willie, what's up? Don't you like lessons?"

"Got the dogs to take out," said Willie, still looking down on the ground.

"Now, see here, Willie," said Mr. Crack, "you take your chance of schooling! Do you think I'd ever be head of a circus like this if I'd never had any schooling? I'll have to send you away from the circus to a proper school, if you're not careful. It's the law of this land that every child should be taught its lessons."

Fenella was scared. She didn't want Willie to be sent away to school. "He'll come, Mr. Crack," she said earnestly. "He's always come before. He's getting on very well."

"Well, my orders are that these two children go to you five mornings a week," said Mr. Crack to Presto. "Hear that, Willie? Now take that scowl off your face and go!"

Mr. Crack strode off looking rather annoyed. Sulking made him angry. "A sulky animal or a sulky human being will never do anything worth while!" he always said. "If I get hold of an animal that goes into the sulks, I never bother with it again. It's no use to me."

Willie was not very nice that morning. Fenella tried to talk to him and cheer him up, but he was still in the sulks. Presto was patient with him. Fenella tried to make up for Willie's behaviour by working extra well—but that didn't please Willie either.

"Sucking up to him!" he whispered to Fenella crossly. "Just because you know I'm doing badly, you try to suck up to him and do extra well!"

"You're horrid, Willie!" said Fenella, almost in tears, for she couldn't bear Willie, her cheerful friend, to be like this.

Presto took no more notice of Willie, but set him some writing to do, and began to teach Fenella geography from a big globe he brought from a corner. She learnt quickly and well and he was pleased with her.

"I'm awfully thirsty," said Fenella, when lessons had finished. "I really must get a drink!"

"Here is one," said Presto, and gave her a jug and a cup. "Pour it out for yourself."

She began to pour from the jug—and then she almost dropped the cup! "Oh!" she cried, "I've poured two tiny goldfish into the cup from the jug. But they weren't in the jug, Mr. Presto, or I'd have seen them. How did they get into the cup?"

"Dear, dear!" said Presto, and poured the water from the cup back into the jug. Fenella peered into it. There were no goldfish to be seen.

"Now pour it out again," said Presto. "I hope this time the water will be clear!"

But it wasn't! The goldfish appeared again in the cup, although Fenella was quite certain they were not in the jug when she poured out the water. She stared at Presto in wonder.

"You really are magic!" she said. "What shall I do? I can't drink the goldfish."

"You will have to go and get a drink from your aunt, I'm afraid," said Presto, in a regretful voice. "I'm so sorry. It does sometimes happen to me that goldfish appear in my drinking water."

Fenella went off puzzled. Willie followed. He looked more cheerful now that lessons were over.

"Isn't Presto clever?" said Fenella. "Last time we had lessons he kept making my rubber disappear, and I kept finding that I was sitting on it. This time there are goldfish in his drinking water. Oh, Willie—I think we're lucky to have lessons with a conjurer. Don't you?"

"No," said Willie, going gloomy again. "Lessons with anyone are awful. I shall never learn to read."

"Willie, do let me help you," begged Fenella. "You always say you've got things to do when I come to see you in the evenings with our books."

"Well, I'll see," said Willie. "What's the time? Hurrah! Presto must have let us off early. We've got time to take the dogs down to the shore. Come on!"

The dogs went nearly mad with joy at being taken down to the fine stretch of sand by the sea. They tore down the little path that wound down the cliff-side, almost knocking over Mrs. Connie who had been down for a paddle.

The children left Cackles and Bobbo behind. They meant to take them down to the sea after tea. Fenella jumped the last bit of the path down, and landed on the firm golden sand. She stared round.

"Oh, Willie! It's lovely! Look at the shiny shells everywhere in the sand. And do see the tiny, lacy waves curling over at the edge. Quick, let's take off our shoes!"

106

They were soon paddling, shouting merrily to one another. Willie had quite forgotten his sulks. The dogs raced one another, and some of them splashed boldly into the sea, barking bravely at the waves.

"Aren't the dogs enjoying themselves?" said Willie. "Hey, Pickles! Fetch this stick. Let's see if you can swim."

"Yes, of course he can," said Fenella, watching the little dog swimming after the floating stick. "Oh, Willie, I want a swim, too. Let's bathe to-morrow. No, let's bathe after tea! Have you got a bathing suit?"

"No, but Micko has," said Willie. "He'll lend me it. What about you?"

"I haven't got one either, but I'm sure I can quickly make one this afternoon, if Aunt Lou will let me," said Fenella joyfully. "Oh, look at Bouncer—he's sniffing at that crab. There, I knew he'd get a pinch! Come away, Bouncer, or you'll get another!"

That afternoon Fenella sat down to help her aunt with the usual pile of sewing. They were busy on Mr. Holla's new suit. It was to be made of the gay, red cloth that Aunt Lou had bought in the town.

Aunt Lou cut it out cleverly from a pattern. She began to tack it together. "You can sew up these seams," she said.

"Oh, I do wish we had a sewing-machine," said Fenella. "We could do all this so much more quickly then."

"I've never had one," said Aunt Lou. "And it's not likely you will, either, Fenella, so just get on with the seams as quickly as you can."

When they were almost finished, and the suit was ready for Mr. Holla to try on, Fenella remembered to ask about a bathing dress for herself.

"Aunt Lou, I do want to bathe this evening after tea. I can swim, you know. Willie can't, so I'll teach him. Is there a bit of stuff I can have for a bathing dress?"

"No, I've nothing that will do," said Aunt Lou. "Nothing at all."

She saw the little girl's disappointed face, and rose suddenly. She went to a little trunk at the back of the caravan and opened it. She delved down into it, felt about for a moment and then brought up a beautiful little bathing suit in pure white, with a shiny belt of bright red.

"You can have this," said Aunt Lou, and gave it to Fenella. "You've been a good girl to help me so well this afternoon."

She did not wait to be thanked but went out of the caravan at once. Fenella stared at the little suit in delight. It would just fit her! How kind of Aunt Lou.

She sat and thought for a minute. Whose was this little suit? Uncle Ursie came into the caravan to get his pipe and saw Fenella sitting there. "You hurry up and get out of doors," he said. "It's lovely out. Had your tea?"

"Yes, we had it whilst we were sewing," said Fenella. Uncle Ursie went out. Fenella undressed quickly and put on the bathing dress. It fitted her perfectly. She ran down the steps to find Willie.

Uncle Ursie was outside, smoking. He looked up—and then his face wrinkled up in astonishment. He stared at Fenella. "Where did you get that suit?" he asked at last.

"Aunt Lou gave it to me," said Fenella. "Why do you look so surprised, Uncle?"

"Well—that suit was our little Carol's," said Uncle Ursie. "Why, Fenny—your aunt must be fond of you to lend you that! But don't you let her see you in it, or she may be sorry she's lent it you, and want it back."

"Then I'll go and bathe now," said Fenella, anxious to keep the lovely little suit. "Willie! Come along quickly! I'll get Bobbo, and we'll go down to the sea."

A LOT OF FUN—BUT JIMMY IS NAUGHTY

WILLIE, Fenella, Bobbo, and Cackles made their way down the little cliff path. Bobbo had to be helped.

"He might roll all the way down if he fell, he's so fat," said Fenella anxiously.

"He wouldn't hurt himself," said Willie. "His fur is so thick! Come on, Cackles. Don't be so slow."

Cackles suddenly spread her great white wings and flew down to the shore. Willie grinned. "Good for Cackles! She got out of scrambling down over these rocks, and I don't wonder!"

Soon they were all dancing about in the waves at the edge of the water. Willie had borrowed Micko's bathing trunks. His body seemed very white indeed, compared with his brown face, neck and arms. Fenella laughed at him and splashed him. He splashed her back and she squealed.

Cackles paddled solemnly, too, occasionally giving a cackle of joy. Then she suddenly waded in much deeper, and launched herself like a battleship, gliding off beautifully.

"She's using her great feet like paddles to get along with," cried Fenella, following her. "Come out deeper, Willie. Do!"

But neither Willie nor Bobbo would go out very far. Bobbo was not really sure if he liked this curious water, that seemed to run after him, and then run away from him—and then, as soon as he went cautiously near it again, ran after him once more. Willie, who couldn't swim, was afraid of getting out of his depth.

So Fenella swam after Cackles the goose. "Oh, Cackles, isn't it lovely?" she cried. "I'd like a ride on your back. Cackles, will you let me? You're big enough to carry me."

But Cackles didn't understand, or didn't want Fenella

to ride her. She kept slipping away when Fenella tried to hold her. Willie yelled with laughter.

"I'll buy you an ice cream, Fenny, if you can ride Cackles! "

But Fenella couldn't win that ice cream! Just when she thought she really had got on to Cackles' broad white back, the goose dived under the water, and down went Fenella, too, gasping and spluttering. Willie lay down in the water and laughed, kicking his legs up into the air, much to the interest of Bobbo, who couldn't imagine what Willie was doing. He came cautiously nearer to see. Then he sat down with a bump beside Willie, lay down himself, and kicked, too, grunting happily, and splashing Willie. Willie sat up.

"Fenny, look at Bobbo! Isn't he a clown? Really, he'd bring the house down if he went in the ring and did this sort of thing! We really ought to teach him a few tricks."

Bobbo rolled over and over in the water. He was enjoying himself very much. Then he gave another grunt and sat up. He looked up the shore and grunted again.

The children looked, too. A small figure was skipping down towards them, dressed in tiny shorts and a little coat and hat.

"Oh, it's one of Mrs. Connie's monkeys! " said Fenella. "He must have seen us from the cliff and come to join us."

"It's Jimmy," said Willie. "Hey, Jimmy! Do you want to paddle?"

Jimmy didn't only want to paddle. He wanted to bathe like the others. With joyful chattering he began to tear off his clothes. Away went his shorts in the wind, and away went his jacket! His cap went sailing away on the strong breeze, too.

"Jimmy! You mustn't do that! " cried Willie. "Oh, look, Fenny, the wind has taken all Jimmy's clothes and blown them out to sea. Can you get them?"

"I'll try," said Fenella and began to swim after them.

But she couldn't get them. They soon became soaked with water and vanished.

Fenella swam back to Willie out of breath. "Will Mrs. Connie be cross?" she asked. "It really wasn't our fault. Oh, do look at Jimmy. He's splashing Bobbo. Aren't they funny together?"

Willie was shivering. He hadn't kept himself warm with swimming as Fenella had. "Come on out," said Fenella. "You'll get a chill. Brrrrrr! I wish we'd brought towels down with us. Anyway, the climb up the cliff will soon warm us."

"Come on, Cackles," yelled Willie. The goose had seen that the others were ready to go, and was already swimming towards them. She waddled out of the water, shaking hundreds of silvery drops over the children. Then Bobbo got up and shook himself, too. Jimmy leapt about like a mad thing, and wouldn't be caught.

"We'll have to leave him if he won't come," said Willie, shivering more than ever. "Come along, Fenny."

But as soon as they all started up the steep cliff path Jimmy came, too, scampering behind them, sometimes on all-fours, sometimes on his hind legs, chattering loudly.

"Shall I tell Mrs. Connie about Jimmy's lost clothes, or will you?" asked Fenella.

"I will," said Willie kindly. "I know you'd be scared of telling her. Anyway, she can't eat us for it! It really wasn't our fault. Jimmy simply tore them off and threw them away!"

Willie went off to dry himself and dress. He said he would find Mrs. Connie as soon as he got his clothes on. Fenella ran to her own caravan and was soon dry, and dressed, with an extra coat on till she felt really warm.

Aunt Lou and Uncle Ursie were talking to Fric and Frac at the other end of the field. Aunt Lou had Mr. Holla's new suit over her arm. She had been fitting it on Mr. Holla, and he was very pleased with it. Now it had only small alterations to be done, and buttons and braid to be sewn on.

Fenella skipped over to them. She looked at the tall, straight Fric and Frac, two brothers who came from Russia, and who were really wonderful horsemen. She thought she liked them best in their Red Indian costumes, even though they did look very fierce then.

Willie went to find Mrs. Connie as soon as he was dressed, but she was not in her caravan. He peeped inside the monkeys' caravan. They were all there but Jimmy. Where could that little rascal be? Well, he would have to wait till Mrs. Connie came back before he could explain what had happened to Jimmy's clothes.

Jimmy the monkey was feeling scared. He was so used to wearing clothes that he felt queer without them now. The wind blew and he wished he had his little coat on. He went and sat on the top of Aunt Lou's caravan, hugging the chimney, which was warm. He saw Fenella slip in, in her bathing costume. He saw her slip out again and go over to the other end of the field.

Jimmy slid down the side of the red caravan and peeped in at the window. On a shelf he saw Rosebud lying, smiling her stiff doll-like smile. Jimmy looked at her for a long time. He couldn't understand that doll. She looked alive, but she never spoke or moved.

But she had beautiful clothes! Jimmy took a quick look round and then disappeared inside the window. He went over to Rosebud. He tugged at her coat, but it wouldn't come off because it was done up with hooks and eyes, and Jimmy was only used to buttons.

Then he saw a small trunk beside Rosebud. In it, neatly packed, was all the doll's wardrobe—coats, dresses, petticoats, vests, everything that Fenella had made for her herself. The monkey shook out each little garment and looked at it, chattering to himself in a low voice.

He found a red silk frock. It was very beautiful and soft, and Jimmy loved red. He pulled it about and then slipped it over his head. He pulled it down straight, and felt pleased. Now he was dressed again. He was grand!

Jimmy scampered away from Grin

He found a white coat edged with fur. Jimmy knew how to put his little arms in to sleeves, for Mrs. Connie had taught him that. He soon had the coat on. It was back to front, but Jimmy didn't mind that! He capered about the caravan, feeling very pleased with himself.

He went back to the trunk again. He saw some red shoes there, and he pulled them out. He fitted them on his little hind paws, and did up the buttons. These took him a long time, but he was a very persevering little monkey indeed. At last the buttons were done up. Now for a hat!

Rosebud's best hat was wrapped up in tissue paper. Jimmy tore off the wrapping. Ah, what a hat! It was made of straw, with bright red roses all round it, and a blue ribbon floating down the back. Rosebud looked really sweet in it when she wore it. Fenella had made it for her on her last birthday.

Jimmy put it on. He didn't know which was back and which was front, so he just jammed it on anyhow, and the blue ribbon hung down over his right ear.

The monkey heard a noise outside and crouched down in a corner. It was Uncle Ursie passing. Jimmy waited till he was gone, then scampered out of the caravan. He looked a very peculiar sight, rather like an ugly doll come alive, all dressed up!

Mr. Holla saw him first. "Hey!" he cried, seeing Jimmy sitting on the top of a caravan. "Who's that?"

Willie and Fenella ran up. "It's one of Mrs. Connie's monkeys," said Willie. "How she has dressed him up! I've never seen one in that costume before!"

Fenella gave a loud squeal. "Oh! It must be Jimmy. The bad, bad monkey! He's got at Rosebud's trunk of clothes, and he's dressed himself up in her best things. Oh, oh, Willie, get him before he spoils them all!"

But Jimmy knew very well that his lovely new clothes would be taken away from him if he was caught, so he led everyone a very fine dance indeed. He bounded about, chattering and squealing. In the end Grin caught him—and spanked him, too, much to Jimmy's dismay.

Fenella was almost crying. "Oh, Rosebud's beautiful clothes! Oh, Aunt Lou, he's torn the frock—and the hat is spoilt!"

Mrs. Connie arrived just then. When she heard what Jimmy had done she threw back her head and laughed. "Ah, that Jimmy! He is the naughtiest and cleverest monkey in the world! What has he done with his own clothes?"

Fenella was cross. Mrs. Connie shouldn't have laughed like that. "He came down to bathe with Willie and me, and he took off all his clothes and threw them away into the water," she said.

Mrs. Connie stopped laughing. This was serious. "What! He has no clothes! Then what will he do when we give our next show? He must have clothes for that!"

Aunt Lou looked grim. "Well, it's no use coming to *me* for them, Mrs. Connie. I'm not making any more clothes for your monkeys, I can tell you that! You shouldn't leave your creatures loose when you go out."

"I didn't! That Jimmy must have squeezed himself out through the chimney!" said Mrs. Connie. "What am I to do? He must have clothes, he must!"

WILLIE AND FENELLA MAKE A PLAN

THE circus folk told the story of mischievous Jimmy over and over again, and everyone laughed. "That Jimmy! He is as clever as a whole bagful of monkeys!" they said.

Aunt Lou kept her word about not making new clothes for Jimmy. "No," she said, when Mrs. Connie came to her about it. "I'm not paid to dress your monkeys, as I've told you before—and why should I work my fingers to the bone, sewing clothes for animals, when all they do is to throw them off into the sea!"

"He didn't know what he was doing," pleaded Mrs. Connie. "You know what monkeys are. Lou, make him a new suit. He can't go into the ring undressed. Some of the others want new things, too."

"They can want then," said Aunt Lou grimly. "Or you can for once in a way put a thimble on your finger and take a needle and thread, and do a bit of work yourself!"

"You're a hard one!" said Mrs. Connie. "Yes, you are! Hard on your old Ursie, and hard on Fenny here. Not a bit of softness or affection for anyone. You listen to me, Fenny—when you've had enough of that hard old aunt of yours, you come to me, see! I'll let you live in my caravan with me, and you can help to look after my precious monkeys."

"I shouldn't let Fenella go even if she wanted to," said Aunt Lou, angrily. "She's in our charge. Now go away and look after those awful monkeys of yours a bit better."

Fenella was sorry for Mrs. Connie. She had quite forgiven Jimmy for taking Rosebud's clothes. She knew that the monkey hadn't really meant to be naughty. She spoke to her aunt.

"Will Mrs. Connie go to Mr. Crack, Aunt Lou? Will she tell him you won't make things for the monkeys? You make them for Grin and Bearit, and for Cackles the goose."

"She can go if she likes," said Aunt Lou. "But I'm not obeying even Mr. Carl Crack if I don't want to. He can turn me and your uncle out of his circus if he likes. I shan't change my mind about those monkeys."

"Oh, Aunt *Lou*! Could he really turn you out?" said Fenella in horror. "Make you and Uncle Ursie—and me, too—go away from the camp and not come back? What would we do?"

"Why—would you mind so much?" asked Uncle Ursie, who had just come into the caravan. "You've not been with us more than two or three weeks!"

"Oh, Uncle Ursie—I'd hate to leave!" cried Fenella.

"I love this caravan—and the bears—and everyone—especially Willie and Cackles. Oh, please, Aunt Lou, do make dresses for the monkeys. I'm sure Mrs. Connie will go to Mr. Crack and he'll say you are to; and if you won't, we'll be turned out."

"It's true that Mr. Crack will not have anyone going against his orders," said Uncle Ursie. "There's been one or two who have—and they've been yelled at and turned out of the camp in a few hours."

Mrs. Connie did go to Mr. Crack. He frowned as he heard her complaint. "'Tisn't just this time, Mr. Crack, sir—it's many a time she's complained about dressing my monkeys. She and I, sir, we can't live in the same circus much longer. I'll go. I'll go somewhere where there's people who'll think more of me, and dress my monkeys as befits them, the little clever creatures."

Mr. Crack didn't like Aunt Lou. He thought her a bad-tempered, scold of a woman. Few people had a good word to say of her.

"She used to be nicer," he said to Mrs. Connie. "Perhaps that was before you joined us, Connie. She changed when she lost Carol. That was her little girl, you know—the cleverest little thing you ever saw! She had a mane of red hair like Fenella's."

"What happened to her?" asked Mrs. Connie.

"Well, Carol was a fine swimmer," said Mr. Crack. "In those days Ursie used to have performing seals, too, and Carol used to go into their tank with them, and do all kinds of tricks. Clever as paint, she was! She could even stand up and ride on a seal's back—and that's a slippery trick to do if you like!"

"My, she must have been clever," said Mrs. Connie.

"Well, Carol got a chill one day," said Mr. Crack, "and instead of keeping her warm in bed and fussing her a bit, Lou let her go to the show as usual, and swim in the seal's tank. The water was cold. The child fell very ill afterwards, and she died. People blamed Lou very much for it, and she changed after that, grew bad-tempered, and never let anyone mention Carol's name."

"Poor Lou!" said Mrs. Connie. "What happened to the seals?"

"She made Ursie sell them, so now he's only got his bears," said Mr. Crack. "I'm fond of Ursie, and if it wasn't for him, and the fact that Lou is a wonder at making show clothes, I'd have got rid of her long ago. Well, Connie, I'll give orders that she's to dress Jimmy from head to foot. If she doesn't, out they go!"

Mrs. Connie was now half sorry that she had come to Mr. Crack with her complaint. She hadn't heard all Lou's story before. She, too, liked Ursie. "Well," she began, "maybe I can get my sister in to help with the monkeys' clothes, Mr. Crack."

Mr. Crack frowned till his shaggy eyebrows hid his eyes completely. "I've said what's to be done," he told Mrs. Connie. "I never change my mind. You know that."

He walked over to the red caravan the next day. Uncle Ursie was there, and Fenella. Aunt Lou had gone by bus to get something she wanted in the town.

"Morning, Ursie," said Mr. Crack. "Where's Lou? Tell her when she comes back that my orders are that she dresses those monkeys as usual—and she's to make a new outfit for Jimmy, top to toe!"

Uncle Ursie looked very troubled. "Yes, Mr. Crack, sir, I'll tell her. But you know what Lou is—so obstinate when she's made up her mind about anything. I doubt if she will do as you say."

"I, too, am obstinate!" suddenly roared Mr. Crack, and made Fenella almost jump out of her skin. "If she disobeys me—out she goes and you with her!"

Fenella began to tremble. She did so hate people to roar and bellow and lose their tempers. She felt quite certain that Aunt Lou would refuse to do what she was ordered.

And so she did. "I'm not changing my mind," she said to Uncle Ursie, when he told her what Mr. Crack had said, and she looked grimmer than ever. Her lips

118

almost disappeared, she screwed her mouth up so tightly. "He can turn us out if he wants to."

Fenella was very unhappy that day. She didn't pay much attention to her lessons and Presto scolded her for the first time. Willie looked at the gloomy little girl in surprise. "What's up?" he whispered.

"No whispering," said Presto. "Pay attention to your work. I am not pleased with either of you this morning."

The two children were impatient to be out of the black caravan. It was not a very nice day, cloudy, and still very windy. When Presto said they might go, they ran to a big lorry full of benches, and squeezed underneath it, finding shelter from the wind. "Now you tell me what's the matter?" said Willie. "I've never seen you look so gloomy before! "

Fenella told him. "So it looks as if we might be turned out of the camp in a few days," she said, tears in her eyes. "And I don't want to go, Willie. I don't want never to see you and Cackles again."

Willie gave her a squeeze. He thought for a few moments. Then he turned to Fenny. "Could *you* make a new suit for Jimmy, top to toe?" he asked.

"Why yes, I suppose so," said Fenella in surprise. "But why?"

"Well, silly, that's a way out of the difficulty, isn't it?" said Willie. "All you need to do is to make the new suit without anyone seeing you—pack it up neatly—and leave it in Mrs. Connie's caravan sometime, with Jimmy's name on it. She'll find it, think your aunt has made it, report it to Mr. Crack—he'll be pleased, and nothing more will be said! "

"Oh," said Fenella, blinking away her tears. "What an idea, Willie! Do you really think it would work? It couldn't be wrong to do that, could it?"

"Well, it's going to please a whole lot of people," said Willie. "It'll please Mrs. Connie—it'll please Mr. Crack—and Jimmy the monkey! It'll please your aunt and uncle when Mr. Crack doesn't turn them out—and it'll certainly please me, too! "

119

"Oh, and me as well!" said Fenella. Her eyes shone. "I could easily make a suit for Jimmy—a little red soldier suit, Willie. But where will I get the stuff for it? And where can I make it so that no one will see me?"

"My mum's got plenty of old stuff you can use," said Willie. "She was once an acrobat, you know, and had pretty dresses like Malvina and the others. She's kept them all. I'm sure she'd let you have one to cut up."

Fenella simply couldn't imagine the thin, worn Aunt Aggie dressed in beautiful clothes and performing in the ring as an acrobat. "Where shall I make Jimmy's suit?" she said. "I mustn't let Aunt Lou or Mrs. Connie see me."

"You can come to our caravan in the evenings," said Willie. "You were going to bring books and help me to read, weren't you? Well, everyone will think that's what we're doing—studying together. And I really will do some work, Fenny, see? Just to please you. We'll have to let Mum into the secret but you needn't mind that. She'll never give us away."

Fenella felt pleased and relieved. Surely, if Mrs. Connie found a beautifully-made little suit for Jimmy in her caravan, everything would be all right?

A seagull swooped down over the cliff and called loudly, "Eee-ooo, eee-ooo!" Willie immediately imitated it.

"Eeee-ooo, eeee-ooo!" he called. The gull heard him and flew down to the ground. Willie went on calling and calling, and one by one more gulls dropped down to the ground in surprise. They thought that surely one of their number must be in distress, under the caravan.

"Eee-oo, eee-oo, eeeeoooo!" they called, and began to circle round and swoop down by the dozen. Willie and Fenella laughed to see them!

The circus folk wondered at the enormous collection of gulls that had suddenly appeared. Then Mr. Holla caught sight of Willie under the caravan.

"Ho, it's you!" he said. "You must imitate gulls in

our next show, Willie! You will bring them into the tent, and everyone will clap! That will be a good trick to play."

Willie and Fenella crawled out, laughing. The gulls flew away. Cackles waddled up, looking indignant. She had not liked so many big birds about in *her* field.

"Oh, Cackles! We've got a secret!" said Fenella. "But we're not going to tell it even to *you*!"

FENELLA SETS TO WORK— WHERE IS BOBBO?

THAT evening Fenella went to Aunt Aggie's caravan with two reading books. Her Aunt Lou saw her go. "Are you going to help Willie with his reading?" she said. "That's good of you, Fenella. If they ask you to stay to supper, you can, because your uncle and I are going out."

Fenella was pleased. She was sure that Willie's mother would ask her to stay. She was quite a favourite with her. Now she would have a really long time to start on Jimmy's new suit!

Willie had told his mother all about their secret. She listened in silence. "Well, Willie," she said, "I like old Lou, for all her sharp tongue. She's a sad woman under her grimness and scolding. She loved that girl of hers very much and blamed herself for her illness. She'd be miserable away from Mr. Crack's circus. She's been with it for years and years. I'll find some stuff for little Fenny to sew up, and if Mrs. Connie takes the suit and says nothing, well, that's all to the good. Lou won't have to go, and we'll have little Fenny with us still. I'm really fond of that red-haired child."

Fenella came in smiling. "Willie, I've brought your books," she said. "Has he told you our secret, Aunt Aggie? Are you going to help me? Oh, good! Now,

121

Willie, you're to sit down and read out loud to me, whilst I get on with my job!"

"All right, Aunt Lou-Fenella," said Willie with a grin and everyone laughed. Aunt Aggie pulled some bright red silk out of a box. "This was once a skirt of mine," she said. "I wore it when I worked with three acrobats, and it was so pretty I've never had the heart to part with it. It's getting on for twenty years old, that skirt—but maybe it's still good enough for you to use, Fenny!"

Fenny fingered the thick red silk. "Oh, it's lovely!" she said. "Thank you, Aunt Aggie. Can I really cut it up?"

"Well, *I'll* never use it again!" said Aunt Aggie with a sigh. "I'm spry enough for my age, but I'd never be able to work in the ring again. You have it, my dear."

Fenella set to work. She glanced at Willie. "Go on!" she said. "Begin your reading! You don't want to be bottom of my class, do you?"

Willie grinned and began to read, very haltingly. But he was certainly beginning to get better. Fenella corrected his mistakes, as she busily began cutting out. Aunt Aggie watched her in admiration.

"How you can cut out that little coat—and listen to Willie reading at the same time and put him right when he goes wrong—beats me! I'll have to get you to teach me to read, too, Fenny."

Fenella stopped her work in amazement. She stared at Aunt Aggie. "Can't *you* read?" she said. "Goodness! Of course I'll teach you, if you like."

"You're a clever little girl," said Aunt Aggie; and the praise was sweet to Fenella, for she got very little of it from her Aunt Lou.

She knew Jimmy's measurements because she had seen her doll's clothes on him. She cut out trousers and coat, and then asked Aunt Aggie if she had cardboard she could use to make him a round, red, pill-box hat, such as soldiers used to wear.

"I could cover it with red," she said. "And, oh, Aunt Aggie, is that gold braid I can see in that box? May I

122

use that, too? I can make his soldier suit look awfully smart with that!"

Fenella got on very well indeed that evening. She enjoyed the time very much. It was fun to hear Willie reading and making mistakes she could put right. It was exciting making such a fine little soldier suit for Jimmy. It was nice to have supper with two people she liked, sitting on the caravan steps with Cackles just below to rest her feet on.

"I wish I lived with you and your mother," she said to Willie. And she thought to herself that she would soon tidy up and clean the dirty caravan, mend all Willie's clothes, and his mother's, too, and make new curtains to take the place of the ragged ones at the window.

"I must go now," she said at last. "I've had a lovely evening, really lovely. The suit has just got to have the gold braid on it, that's all, and the buttons, if you can find me some, Aunt Aggie. Little brass ones, if you can find any. I'll cover the hat to-morrow, too, if I've got time."

Bobbo whimpered as Fenella went by his cage. She hadn't taken him with her that evening, and he missed her. She looked into the big cage. "Bobbo!" she said. "Are you lonely? I'll go and ask Uncle Ursie if I can play with you for a bit."

She went to the red caravan. There was no one there. Of course—Aunt Lou and Uncle Ursie were out. She saw the key of the bears' caravan hanging up on its nail. She took it down.

"I'm sure Uncle Ursie wouldn't mind if I took Bobbo into the caravan to play with him for a bit," thought Fenella. "I'll be careful to lock the door after me, so that Clump can't get out."

She took the key and went to the cage. It was almost dark now, and she couldn't see where Bobbo was. But he could see Fenella all right! He was waiting at the door for her eagerly, a little soft, round barrel of a bear, whimpering for his friend. Clump took no notice. He had had a good meal, and was sleepy.

Fenella took Bobbo out, and locked the cage door carefully. Then she lifted Bobbo into her arms and walked with him to the caravan. "You're growing," she said. "You're getting heavy, Bobbo. Don't grow too fast, or I won't be able to lift you. Now, here we are. We'll play a game, shall we?"

But it was almost too dark to play. Fenella looked at the oil lamp that stood on its shelf. Should she light it? She never had, and she was rather afraid of it. She didn't like the big "plop" it made when it was lighted.

"I won't light it," she said to the bear. "You can just sit in my lap and I'll tell you a story."

Bobbo didn't care what they did so long as he was with his friend, Fenella. She sat him on her knee, cuddled him, and began to tell him the story of the Three Bears. She thought that would be a very good tale for him.

When she had finished she felt hungry. It must be getting late! She went to the little larder and opened it. She felt about on the shelf. There was some bread and butter there, and a jar of honey. Good! Bobbo would like that, too.

She had put Bobbo down on her bunk when she went to fetch the food When she went over to him, he had fallen fast asleep! "Oh, I wish I could see what you look like, asleep in my bunk!" said Fenella. She clambered up beside him, and ate the bread and honey. Then, feeling tired, she cuddled down beside the warm, soft little bear.

"I must take you back and go to bed, Bobbo," she said sleepily. "I—really—must!"

But in half a second Fenella was asleep, too! She was very tired, and she slept as soundly as the little bear, cuddled up close to her.

Aunt Lou and Uncle Ursie came back by the last bus. They walked through the field gate and made their way to their caravan. "I'll just see if the bears are all right," said Uncle Ursie. He always went to look at them last thing, before he went to bed. He put his hand inside the dark caravan and felt about for his keys.

He took the one belonging to the bears' cage and went over to it. He unlocked the door and went in. He switched on his torch and spoke softly to the bears.

"Clump! Bobbo! Are you all right?"

Clump answered him with a grunt. He was curled up in his favourite corner. Uncle Ursie kicked the straw from the heap in the other corner, expecting to see Bobbo curled up there. But he wasn't, of course.

Uncle Ursie looked round the cage in alarm. Where was Bobbo? He wasn't anywhere to be seen! He wasn't in the cage at all!

Uncle Ursie, puzzled and upset, locked the cage door and went to Aunt Lou. "Bobbo's not there," he said. "He's gone! Someone must have taken him! Or do you think he can possibly have squeezed through the bars?"

"Oh, Ursie!" said Aunt Lou. "No, surely he couldn't have done that. He's too fat. Besides, he would have got out before now if he *could* have squeezed through the bars!"

The caravan was still dark. Aunt Lou hadn't lighted the lamp for fear of waking Fenella. She had felt for the little girl in the bunk, but had not touched furry Bobbo.

"I'd better rouse the camp," said Uncle Ursie. "Bobbo's too valuable to lose like this. Besides, he'll be terrified. I'll get Holla and Tiny. Wriggle will help to search, too."

He set off to the caravans belonging to the three men. They were all in their bunks and asleep. They got up at once when they heard Ursie's news, and pulled on their trousers and jerseys.

"We haven't seen him wandering about," said Holla. "He *must* be in his cage, Ursie. Maybe he's curled up with Clump. It's impossible for him to get out."

"Well—we'll have another look if you like," said Uncle

Ursie, and they went back to Clump's cage. But no, was quite certain there was no Bobbo in with him.

"We'd better separate and go round the camp to search," said Holla. But just then there came a low call from the red caravan. It was Aunt Lou.

"Come here a minute!" she said. They all came up the steps. "Come right in," she said, and switched a bright torch on to Fenella's bunk. The four men stared.

For there, lying tightly curled up together, their arms round one another, were Fenella and the lost bear! They were both sound asleep.

Mr. Holla chuckled. "Well, well! That little Fenella of yours is a caution! You ought to get her to do something with that young bear, Ursie. She might come into the ring one day with him, if she makes anything of him. They're a pair, I must say!"

Aunt Lou looked rather cross. "I'm sorry Ursie has had to wake you all up," she said. "Fenella's most tiresome to do this. I'll scold her in the morning."

"No, don't," said Wriggle hastily. "She meant no harm. I don't mind being waked up, when I see that sight—Fenny and the bear!"

The men went back to their caravans, all chuckling at Fenella and the bear. Ursie tried to pacify Aunt Lou. He took the sleeping bear gently away from Fenella and put him in his cage with Clump. Fenella didn't stir.

"Now don't you get cross with her to-morrow," said Uncle Ursie when he came back. "She's a good little thing really. You give her a few smiles, Lou, instead of harsh words. I might have guessed where Bobbo was! I will another time!"

LESSONS FOR WILLIE, FENELLA AND BOBBO!

THE next morning, rather to Uncle Ursie's surprise, Aunt Lou did not scold Fenella very hard for what had happened the night before.

Fenella was sorry when she heard how upset Uncle Ursie had been, and how he had waked up Mr. Holla, Mr. Tiny and Mr. Wriggle to help him look for the bear.

"And all the time he was curled up with me, fast asleep," said Fenella. "Oh, Uncle Ursie, I must have fallen asleep without meaning to. I'm so sorry."

"It's not good to do things that cause trouble to other people," said Aunt Lou; but that was about all she said. Fenella went to say she was sorry to Mr. Holla and the others.

"Oh, don't mind about *that*," said Mr. Holla. "I never mind being waked up in the middle of the night!"

Mr. Tiny had taken his elephants down to the sea for a bathe, so she couldn't speak to him. But she found Mr. Wriggle in his caravan.

"I'm sorry you were waked up last night all because of me," she told him. Wriggle said he didn't mind at all, he rather liked it.

"It was nice of you to come and say you're sorry," he said. "Not many people do that, you know. As a reward I'll tread on my head for you."

"Oh *no*, thank you all the same," said Fenella hurriedly. "Mr. Wriggle, you know I don't want to see you do that. Oh, please don't!"

Mr. Wriggle was doing such alarming wriggles and bends and twists that Fenella really did think he would end in treading on his own head. She ran off quickly to find Willie.

"Come along to Presto," she said. "It's time. Willie, did you hear about me and Bobbo last night?"

"Course I did," said Willie. "I guess you got the

rough side of your aunt's tongue this morning."

"No, she didn't say much," said Fenella. "Come on, Cackles—lessons! "

Lessons went well that day. Willie's practice in reading the night before seemed to have helped him. Presto was pleased. "You shall give Willie a present," he said to Fenella. "You have something in your pocket for him."

Fenella put her hand in her pocket. She brought out a tiny china goose, just like Cackles!

"Oh, look, Willie! " she said. "A tiny china goose! And it's for *you*! Mr. Presto, you *are* magic! There was nothing but my hanky in there just now! "

"And what is this that Willie has behind his ear?" said the conjurer. "Aha! A tiny wooden bear! "

Willie felt something behind his ear and put up his hand. Sure enough there was a little wooden bear there! Willie grinned. He handed the bear to Fenella, who was delighted with it.

"Oh, is this for me? Thank you, Mr. Presto! Oh, I do think I'm lucky to have lessons from a conjurer! "

Presto almost smiled, but not quite. He took up their two rubbers, two rulers, two pencils and two pens. Deftly he threw them up into the air so that they circled one by one over his head, and caught them as they came down, sending them up again time after time.

"I wish I could do that," said Fenella. "I do really. I wish you'd put juggling and conjuring on to our lesson time-table, Mr. Presto."

"Ah, those things would take years to teach to you," said Presto, putting everything neatly back on the table again. "You must begin when you are two! "

"Oh, dear—it's too late for me to begin then," said Fenella. "But Bobbo isn't two yet. I could teach him things, couldn't I, Mr. Presto?"

"When a young animal loves and trusts anyone as much as that little Bobbo loves and trusts you, Fenella, you can teach him anything! " said Presto. "He is intelligent, that little bear. He imitates well. You should

128

make him yours, Fenella, and teach him. Then maybe one day you could go into the ring with him, and he will bring pleasure and delight to many boys and girls!"

Fenella's eyes shone. "Oh, Mr. Presto! You don't really mean I could ever go into the ring! Willie, did you hear that? Let's teach Bobbo together. After all, you taught Cackles, didn't you, Willie?"

The two children went out into the sunshine. Cackles was pleased to see them. As usual she had been sitting patiently on the steps waiting for them. Cinders had quite given up trying to stop her. One day when he had refused to move from his favourite seat on the top step Cackles had simply squatted down on him. He had been buried under a cascade of warm feathers, and was frightened almost out of one of his nine lives!

"I'm going to get Bobbo," said Fenella. "I think I'll begin teaching him this very day, Willie. What shall I teach him?"

"He's such a little clown," said Willie. "Teach him clownish tricks. Give him a balloon and see what he does with it."

Fenella sped off to ask Mr. Groggy for one of his lovely big balloons. He gave her three, all ready blown up.

"Let's take Bobbo into the ring and practise with him there," said Willie, peeping into the big tent, which was now up and flapping in the strong breeze. "There's nobody here at the moment."

They took Bobbo into the big ring. He knew it well, of course. Fenella showed him one of the balloons. He remembered how Mr. Groggy so often turned head-over-heels when he carried his balloons. The little bear tried to stand on his head to go head-over-heels, and fell over with a flop. He sat down looking comical, and then stretched out a paw for the balloon.

It bounced away from him. Bobbo got up and followed it. He hadn't enough sense tc hold the string, he tried to pick up the balloon itself.

129

But his paws were not made for picking up balloons. The children roared to see him going after the big balloon, which bounced away every time he pawed it. But suddenly one of Bobbo's claws pierced the rubber and the balloon burst with a loud pop.

Bobbo was amazed and horrified. Where had the lovely balloon gone? Whimpering loudly he ran to Fenella to be comforted, holding out his paws.

"You know, Fenny, we've only got to let him play about like this each day, and give him things like balloons —and perhaps an old doll of yours—and so on—and Bobbo will teach himself! " said Willie. "He's so funny. Oh, Fenny—could you make him that clown's suit you were speaking of? He'd look lovely in that, and he really does act like a clown."

Cackles came into the ring. She looked for her house, but it wasn't there. She went through the red curtains to find it. Bobbo followed her. Cackles found her house, opened the gate, walked up the cardboard path and went in at the front door.

She shut it loudly. Bobbo was surprised. He, too, walked in at the gate and up the path. He pushed at the door, but it was latched shut. He lifted his paw and banged loudly.

"He's knocking at the door! Oh, Cackles, let him in! " cried Fenella in delight. But Cackles wouldn't. This was *her* house, wasn't it? Bears could keep out of it!

But suddenly she opened the door and gave Bobbo a peck that surprised him very much. Then she slammed the door shut again. The children yelled with laughter.

"Fenny! We've only got to let these two do things like this, and they'll bring the house down! " cried Willie. "Why shouldn't you come into the ring with me and Cackles? It would be fun! I could go in and do my bird imitations first—and then you could come in with Bobbo—and he could go and bang at Cackles' front door—and she won't let him in; we could make quite a play of it! "

"Willie! Would you let me come in with you when

130

you do your turn, would you really?" cried Fenella. "Oh, I'd love that. I'd never dare to go in alone with Bobbo. Never. But if I could go when you're there, I wouldn't mind a bit."

"Of course you could," said Willie. "My word, we'd make quite a stir, Fenny. Fenella and her pet bear, Bobbo, Willie Winkie and his pet goose, Cackles! That would look fine on the posters, wouldn't it?"

"Do you suppose I could have a very pretty dress?" said Fenella. "A sort of fairy dress?"

"Have what you like," said Willie. "Look like a princess, or a fairy—or Marigold in the tale of the Three Bears!"

"I'd rather be a fairy, I think, with wings," said Fenella. "I wish Presto had enough magic to make wings fly. Oh, Willie, I do feel excited."

"Well—it's easy to make plans," said Willie. "But it's difficult to get things going. Don't hope too much, because Mr. Crack may think it's a silly idea, and your uncle and aunt may refuse to let you go into the ring, anyhow. And Bobbo may not be so good as we think him."

But it wasn't a bit of good Willie pouring cold water on their plans. Fenella was absolutely sure everything would happen just as she wished it.

"I shall make a clown suit for Bobbo at once," she said. "Aunt Lou will give me the stuff, I'm sure. If not, your mother will! Oh, Willie, shall I earn some money, like you, if I do go into the ring?"

"I expect so," said Willie. "Why, what do you want money for?"

"I want to buy Aunt Lou a sewing-machine," said Fenella. "Then she can sew six times as quickly as she does now, and she won't mind making clothes for the animals as well as the circus folk."

"You're rather a dear, Fenny," said Willie, smiling at the eager little girl. "Giving everybody ice creams as soon as you get a few shillings—and wanting to buy a

131

sewing-machine for that bad-tempered aunt of yours if you earn any money! "

"Look at Bobbo now! " said Fenella. "He's got another balloon. Oh, Willie, he's standing on it. Don't, Bobbo, it'll burst. I'll find you one of the dogs' footballs. You can stand on that."

Bobbo did. He could balance very well. He not only stood on the big ball but by moving his hind paws a little to and fro he made the ball move, with himself on top of it!

"Just like Micko does! " said Willie. "Bobbo, you're a born clown, and a clever one! Come along now, and you, too, Cackles. We shan't get any dinner at all if we stay here much longer! We've had a jolly good morning, Fenny, haven't we?"

THE LITTLE SOLDIER SUIT

THE circus was to have a short holiday before giving its next show. Mr. Crack's performers had been working very hard, and some of them were tired. Also, Mr. Crack wanted the clowns to think of some new tricks, and these had to be practised.

Each performer could book the ring for a certain time each day for any practice he wanted. In the mornings Fric, Frac and Malvina were there with their horses. After them came the clowns, thinking out new jokes and new tricks. Mr. Groggy was very clever at this.

Willie had to ask for a time for himself and Fenella. He went to Mr. Crack, who asked why he wanted the time. Surely Cackles the goose knew her part too well to need more time to rehearse?

"Well, sir, we've got an idea we could work up a turn with little Bobbo the bear and Fenella," explained Willie. "He just adores Fenny, you know."

"That won't be any good," said Mr. Crack, who was not in a very good temper that day. "Fenella hasn't

132

been with the circus more than a few weeks. You ought to know that it takes years to make a performer, Willie! I'd never let Fenella go go into the ring!"

"But, sir," began Willie, "we could——"

Mr. Crack cut him short. "Have the time for practice if you like! But it will be wasted, because I can tell you now, Fenella will not be allowed to go into the ring. She will not be good enough for that. And Bobbo isn't old enough."

"Yes, but . . ." tried Willie again, and Mr. Crack drew his shaggy brows over his deep-set eyes warningly. He was about to yell! He reached out for his famous whip.

Willie didn't stop to finish. He fled! He didn't want that whip curling round his legs. That was what usually happened when anyone argued with Mr. Crack. He went to find Fenella, feeling disappointed.

Fenella listened, and her mouth went down at the corners. "Oh! I do think he might let us try. How horrid of him!"

"Well, he says we can have the time to practise, though it will be wasted because he won't let you or Bobbo into the ring," said Willie. "Do you still want to try and work up a turn with Bobbo and me and Cackles?"

"I won't give up!" said Fenella. "We got the idea, and it's a good one. Let's go on with it even though Mr. Crack is horrid about it. And I shall make Bobbo his clown suit, too, so there!"

Willie laughed. "You're a funny one!" he said. "So scared sometimes, and so determined at other times. All right, we'll try out our idea, even though it comes to nothing. Ask your uncle if we can have Bobbo each day."

Uncle Ursie didn't mind at all. He said it was good for the little bear to play about in the ring and learn all he could whilst he was young.

"It is the only time really to learn anything, when you are young," he said. "It is the same for children as for animals. You can't teach an old dog new tricks, but you can teach a young one all the tricks in the world—if

133

he will only learn them! Some animals are like Fenny —they have eager minds and love learning anything. Others are slow and hate learning. It is of no use to teach them."

"Bobbo is so clever," said Fenella. "Once he has found out how to do something, he does it again and again, Uncle. You should see him trying to balance himself on the dogs' football!"

"Oh, can he do that?" said Uncle Ursie in surprise. "There are some bears who are remarkably clever at such a trick. I have a much bigger ball you can use with Bobbo if you like. One that will be easier for him to walk on."

He rummaged about under the red caravan, and found an old box. He took out a big ball, gaily coloured in red, yellow and blue. It was firm and strong.

"Oh!" said Fenella, pleased, "that will do beautifully for Bobbo. Uncle Ursie, what an exciting box! What is this? And, oh, look at these dear little balls!"

"That's a balancing pole one of my performing seals used to have," said Uncle Ursie, picking it up. "He was called Flippers, Fenny, and he was one of the cleverest animals I ever had to do with. He could balance this pole on the end of his nose, and a ball on top of that! These were the balls he used to play with."

"Oh, I *do* wish you had your seals now," said Fenella. "I should love them."

"Yes, and they'd love you," said Uncle Ursie. "Flippers was so loving that he would follow me all over the camp, if I let him out of his tank, flopping about after me like a great dog. He'd kiss me, too."

"Did Carol, your little girl, like him?" asked Fenella.

"She was a marvel with Flippers and the others," said Uncle Ursie, remembering. "The things she could do! You know, Fenny, though you're not really one of the circus folk, you fit in so well that you might have been with us for years—and you do remind me of our little Carol, the way you get on with the animals—especially my bears."

"I know I can't make up to you for your own little girl," said Fenny shyly. "But I'll try to make up just a bit. It's so kind of you to let me live with you, Uncle Ursie. I didn't want to come at first, you know, but now I'm glad I did. I was dreadfully disappointed when I heard I wasn't to go to Canada with my Aunt Janet."

"Were you really?" said Uncle Ursie. "Now don't you tell your Aunt Lou I said you reminded me of Carol. She wouldn't like it."

"Oh, I won't," said Fenella. "Can I really have this big ball for Bobbo, Uncle? He'll love it."

Bobbo certainly did love that big ball. He seemed to know what it was for immediately he saw it. He ran to it, grunting, and whilst Fenny held it for him he clambered up on it, got his balance, and began to walk it round the ring, very earnest and very pleased.

He fell off with a bump. He sat up looking most surprised, grunting. He got up and went after the ball again. He wasn't going to give up. This was fun. Cackles the goose watched him, and when she saw Willie and Fenella laughing and calling out praise to Bobbo, she wanted to do something, too.

So she waited till Bobbo was once more on the ball, and then she went and pecked him from behind. He fell off at once in surprise, and Cackles hissed in delight. The children roared with laughter.

"Who would ever have thought that a baby bear and goose would act together?" said Willie. "Fenny, you *must* make that clown suit for Bobbo as soon as ever you've finished Jimmy's red soldier suit."

Fenella went to work on the red soldier suit again that evening. She sat in Aunt Aggie's caravan, sewing away, whilst Willie once more read out to her from a book. He was really finding it easier to read now, and he began to realise that if only he would set to work and do a little hard practice in reading he would soon be able to read as well as Fenella.

"That's a really beautiful suit," said Aunt Aggie, admiringly. "As good as anything Lou could make.

135

How grand Jimmy will look in it! Though I must say it's more than that mischievous little monkey deserves. Did you know that he had taught Grin and Bearit to throw things over the cliff, and watch them sail away in the wind?"

"Oh, no! Has he really?" cried Fenella. "Isn't he *naughty*, Aunt Aggie? Though I'm sure that Grin and Bearit could quite well have thought of such a mischievous thing themselves."

"Mr. Holla caught the three of them throwing pails and brushes over the cliff," said Aunt Aggie. "Fric and Frac were very angry about it, because they are what they use for the horses. Mr. Holla made Grin and Bearit go down and fetch every single thing. And as fast as they brought them up Jimmy threw them over the cliff again. Nobody could catch him. I must say I think Mrs. Connie ought to keep him locked up."

"He pines if he's locked up," said Fenella. "She says he would die if she kept him in his cage all day."

"Maybe he would," said Aunt Aggie. "You never know with monkeys."

"Did Mr. Holla punish Grin and Bearit?" asked Willie.

"Of course," said Aunt Aggie. "He took away those dolls they like to play with—their toys—and shut them up in his caravan. I heard them yowling like children."

"Oh, it's such fun to live in a circus camp," said Fenella, her needle flying in and out. "All kinds of things happen every day—things that never never could happen to ordinary people. I'm sure I would never have had a baby bear for a pet if I'd lived all my life long with Aunt Janet. And I wouldn't have wanted one either. Now I can't imagine what it would be like to be without Bobbo."

"That little suit is going to make Jimmy look too smart for words!" said Willie. "Is it finished yet?"

"Yes. I'm just putting a bit of braid round his red hat, and the whole thing's done," said Fenella happily. "There! I'll wrap it up now, and we'll leave it in Mrs.

Connie's caravan when we know she's out, Willie. Then I'll set to work to-morrow on Bobbo's clown suit. Perhaps Aunt Lou will find me some stuff. I can't keep asking you for things, Aunt Aggie."

"Oh, you're welcome," said Aunt Aggie. "And you're such a help to Willie, too, in his lessons. You come to me if there's anything you want."

That evening Willie and Fenella took a parcel across to Mrs. Connie's caravan. She was out, but the door was open. Jimmy was inside, playing with the saucepans on the shelf. He skipped out as soon as he saw Willie and Fenella.

"He just *won't* be caught!" said Fenella. "I'll leave the parcel on Mrs. Connie's bunk. There! It's got Jimmy's name on it, so she'll know who it's for. We'd better shut the door and the windows, Willie, or that monkey of a Jimmy will take off the paper, and dress himself up in the suit and spoil it."

They went out and shut the door behind them. They wondered very much what Mrs. Connie would say when she found the suit.

"I hope it doesn't make any trouble," said Fenella anxiously. "I mean—suppose she thanks Aunt Lou for it—and Aunt Lou thinks I shouldn't have done it—and . . ."

"Oh, don't meet trouble half-way," said Willie. "Come on, let's take Cackles and Bobbo down to the sea for a bathe. It's so awfully hot. Get your bathing suit and I'll borrow Micko's again. We'll have a lovely time splashing about!"

A SURPRISE—AND A SHOCK

A GREAT many things happened the next day. It seemed quite an ordinary day at first. Fenella woke up, had her breakfast, chattered to her aunt, and then began to tidy the caravan.

"You get on with it whilst I go and measure Malvina for her new riding coat," said Aunt Lou. "I'll be back in half an hour. Then it will be time for you to go to Presto for your morning lessons."

She went off. Fenella began to sweep the caravan floor. Uncle Ursie was outside, polishing up the big bright chain he put round Clump when he led him into the ring. Clump was very tame and would not hurt anyone, but many people were afraid if they saw that the bear had no chain on him.

Suddenly Mr. Crack called to Uncle Ursie.

"Hey, Ursie! Here's a letter for you! The postman has just been."

The postman came to the camp each morning and delivered all his circus letters to Mr. Crack, who sorted them out and gave them to the various circus folk—whenever they had a letter, which wasn't very often.

Uncle Ursie was surprised. He took the letter and went back to the caravan with it. He opened it and read it slowly. Then he gave a shout.

"Hey, Fenny! Who do you think this is from? It's from your Aunt Janet! She's in Canada now and very happy—and she's sent you some money she had for you, and forgot to arrange about. She sends you her love, too, and says you must write to her, because she misses you very much."

"Oh, does she say that?" said Fenny, coming down the caravan steps looking pleased. "What money has she sent, Uncle Ursie? How nice of her."

"It's a lot of money. It's twenty pounds," said Uncle Ursie. "I'd better put it in the savings bank for you, Fenny."

"No, you have it, Uncle Ursie, because I'm sure I cost you a lot of money to feed," said Fenella. "I have such a big appetite now!"

"I wouldn't take a penny," said Uncle Ursie. "Not a penny. It's a pleasure to have a little girl like you. And besides, look how hard you work at your sewing, Fenny—you earn your keep and more with your needle!

No, the money is yours to do as you like with. Maybe you'll want to spend it some day."

A wonderful idea came into Fenella's mind. She would buy a sewing-machine for Aunt Lou! That would be a very good return indeed for the kindness she and Uncle Ursie had shown her by taking her to live with them when they really couldn't have wanted her.

"Uncle Ursie—I want some now," she said suddenly. "I want very badly to buy something. Could I have some now?"

"What do you want to buy all of a sudden?" asked Uncle Ursie, amused.

"I can't tell you yet," said Fenella. "But, uncle, I really do promise you that it's something you and Aunt Lou will be very, very pleased about when you know what it is. You can trust me, can't you?"

"Oh, I can trust you all right," said Uncle Ursie. "And, after all, it's your own money. But you can't possibly have it all. How much do you want?"

Fenella wondered how much a sewing-machine would cost. She hadn't any idea at all. Could she get one for five pounds? Or would it be more? She would have to ask Aunt Aggie or Mrs. Connie. They might know.

"I don't quite know how much I would want," said Fenella. "Could you give me five pounds, do you think, Uncle Ursie?"

"That's a terrible lot of money," said Uncle Ursie. "But, yes—you can have it, if you really promise me I shall not be cross at the way it's spent."

He counted out five one-pound notes and gave them to Fenella. She was thrilled. "Now I can buy that sewing-machine!" she thought. "And Aunt Lou will be able to do her work twice as quickly and three times as well! She will be so pleased. I can easily show her how to work it."

"I'll put the money into Rosebud's trunk," she told Uncle Ursie. "I'll keep it there till I go to spend it. Oh, what a surprise, Uncle Ursie! How kind of Aunt Janet to send me the money. I'll write to her this very day. I expect Mr. Presto will let me write a letter in lesson-time. I'll go and fetch Willie now and tell him."

She ran off, longing to tell her news. But Willie was nowhere to be seen. She passed Mrs. Connie on the way and wondered if the monkey woman had tried on Jimmy's new suit yet. Mrs. Connie's face was all smiles. She beckoned to Fenella.

"Would you like to see something?" she asked. "Come and look!" She led the way to her caravan. Sitting on the table, as proud as punch, was Jimmy. He was dressed in his red soldier suit, and it fitted him perfectly! He looked really marvellous! His little round red hat was set on one side of his head, and kept in place by the chin-strap.

"Now isn't that perfect?" said Mrs. Connie happily. "I've never seen Jimmy look so grand. It's the finest suit he's ever had. And I've told him I'll take it away from him and let one of the others wear it, if he isn't good. Aha, he'll be good all right now—won't you Jimmy?"

Jimmy certainly looked a good, well-behaved little monkey that morning. He loved fine clothes, and knew that he looked smart. He chattered a little and then, standing up, he walked up and down the table, showing himself off.

"I'd never have thought it of Lou," said Mrs. Connie. "Making Jimmy such a fine suit, after the words we had, and the way she vowed she'd not make Jimmy a thing. It's really kind of her, and I'm going to tell her so."

"Oh, don't say a word to her," said Fenella, alarmed. "Just don't say anything about it, Mrs. Connie. She—she doesn't expect you to."

"Maybe not! But she's going to get a word of thanks from me whether she wants it or not!" said Mrs. Connie. "And I've made her a cake, too, see, Fenny— One of chocolate, with a banana filling—just what she likes. You'll be having it for tea, I expect."

Fenella was even more alarmed. This would never

do. She didn't want Mrs. Connie to make such a fuss about the suit, because after all, her aunt hadn't made it, and it would be just as well if nothing was said about it at all. Fenella began to wish she hadn't made the suit. But surely Aunt Lou wouldn't be angry with her about it? She had only done it for the best.

She looked at the clock in Mrs. Connie's caravan. "Oh, dear—is that right?" she asked. "It's past ten o'clock. I really must go, Mrs. Connie. But do please not say anything to Aunt Lou about the suit!"

Mrs. Connie was puzzled. Didn't Fenella want her aunt to get the words of thanks due to her? Of *course*, she must go and tell Lou how much she liked the suit. If Lou could turn out to be so kind and generous, Mrs. Connie was going to be the same! There was that lovely chocolate cake to take, too. That would please Lou!

Fenella sped off. Wherever was Willie? He couldn't be in Mr. Presto's caravan, because he always waited for her.

She ran to the dogs' cage. They were not there. She called to Mr. Wriggle, who was nearby.

"Have you seen Willie? I can't find him."

"He went off with the dogs," said Wriggle. "I expect he forgot all about lessons! Not too keen on them, is he? I say—can you stay a moment? I'd like you to see me tread on——"

"Oh, no, thank you!" cried Fenella and ran off. Willie *must* be somewhere about! But no, he wasn't. The dogs were gone and so was Willie. She ran round to Aunt Aggie's caravan to ask her if Willie would be back soon, and bumped into Mr. Crack, who was striding along in his big top boots.

"No, now!" he said. "What a hurricane! What are you in such a hurry for?"

"I'm looking for Willie," said Fenella.

"Aha! It's lesson-time, I suppose," said Mr. Crack, and he looked at his enormous gold watch. "A quarter past ten. Isn't ten o'clock your time? Surely you aren't keeping Mr. Presto waiting?"

"Well," said Fenella, not liking to say that she had been hunting for Willie, "well, you see, er—yes, I'm afraid I *am* a bit late this morning, Mr. Crack. I'll go right away now."

"Where *is* Willie?" suddenly roared Mr. Crack after her. Fenella was struck dumb. She never could say a word when people roared at her. She stared at Mr. Crack in fright. Thank goodness he hadn't got that cracking whip with him.

"Have you lost your tongue?" said Mr. Crack, losing his temper. "I asked you—where *is* Willie?"

"Gone to the shore with the dogs," said Wriggle, strolling up, and taking pity on Fenella's fright. "He will be back soon, I expect."

"Tell him to come to me as soon as he gets back," commanded Mr. Crack, and strode off scowling.

"Oh, dear," said Fenella, looking in dismay at Wriggle. "Now Willie will get into trouble. Oh, what will Mr. Crack say to him?"

"He'll give him a hiding, I expect," said Wriggle. "Well, young Willie ought to have sense enough to obey orders. You'd better go now, or you'll get into trouble, too."

Fenella ran off, very troubled. Presto was waiting impatiently in his caravan. He frowned when he saw Fenella.

"Twenty minutes late!" he said. "I thought you had better manners, Fenella. I am ashamed of you, and you make me feel cross. Where is Willie?"

"I don't know," said poor Fenella. "I'm sorry I'm late, Mr. Presto."

"If it happens again, you will get no more lessons from me," said Presto. "Not one. I will have nothing to do with ungrateful people."

This was dreadful. Fenella tried to settle down to her writing, but she couldn't help thinking and thinking about Willie. In half an hour's time he came in. Fenella looked up at him. He glared at her furiously.

"Beast!" he said. "Telling tales of me! Making me

142

go to Mr. Crack. I suppose you're glad I got a hiding from him! I'll never speak to you again."

"Oh, Willie!" said Fenella and burst into sobs. "I didn't tell tales of you! At least——"

"That is enough," said Presto coldly. "You deserved all you got, Willie, and you know it. Stop crying, Fenella. If you told tales of Willie you deserve to be miserable. If you didn't, then you can explain to Willie afterwards. I will have no more disturbance in here this morning!"

It was a dreadful morning. What with Willie's scowls and Fenella's tears and Presto's coldness the time seemed twice as long as usual. Oh, dear—whatever could Fenny do to put things right with Willie?

THINGS GO WRONG

L ESSONS were over at last. There were no presents for good children that day! Fenella tried to take Willie's arm. "Oh, Willie! I didn't tell tales. I met Mr. Crack when I was looking for you, and I just *said* I was looking for you, but it wasn't tales, really it wasn't."

"Ho! That's what *you* think, you mean little thing!" said Willie. "Anyway, it cost me a hiding, and I've been yelled at by Mr. Crack till I'm almost deaf. I didn't mean to be late. One of the dogs ran off and I had to go and look for him. You might have guessed that—but you're so mean you thought you'd go and tell tales of me."

Fenella began to cry. "Willie, you must believe me. I'm not mean like that. Willie, don't push me off like that, you're horrid."

"So are you," said Willie. "I tell you, I don't want to speak to you again. Keep away from me and Cackles."

"Willie, we're not quarrelling, are we?" said Fenella, scared. "We always said we'd never quarrel. It takes two to make a quarrel. I *won't* quarrel!"

143

"I don't care what you do," said Willie, and walked off. Fenella went slowly to the red caravan, feeling very unhappy. She thought she would tell her Aunt Lou and perhaps get a little comfort.

But no! The day had gone wrong, and it went on and on going wrong, in the way some days have. In the caravan was a very angry Aunt Lou indeed. When Fenella came in, she took the little girl by the shoulders and gave her a hard shake.

"What do you mean by sucking up to Mrs. Connie and making that suit for Jimmy behind my back? You sly little thing—never saying a word to me about it— letting her think I'd made it. As if I'd go back on my word! I said I wouldn't, and I meant it. You're a bad, deceitful girl. I told Mrs. Connie a few things this morning, and she went out of here smiling on the other side of her face, I can tell you!"

Fenella listened in horror. She could hardly say a word, but at last she got a few out. "Oh, Aunt Lou— she only meant to be nice to you—and that cake . . ."

"Ho, that cake! I threw it out to the gulls!" said Aunt Lou, and she looked so hard and unkind that Fenella turned away in despair.

The little girl went to the door, but Aunt Lou called her back. "I've not finished with you yet! What about this money your uncle had for you? You're not going to spend that five pounds, let me tell you! Such waste! And what were you going to spend it on, I'd like to know?"

"It was a secret," said Fenella. "I was sure you and Uncle would be pleased when you knew what it was. Do wait and see, Aunt Lou, before you make up your mind I was going to waste it."

"Well, you won't have it," said Aunt Lou. "However foolish your uncle is, I'm *not*. You can't have any of that money to spend till you're much older."

Fenella went down the steps. What horrid things were happening. Willie angry with her, Presto angry, Mr.

Crack angry, and Aunt Lou furious! And now no doubt Mrs. Connie would be, too.

But surprisingly enough Mrs. Connie wasn't. She saw Fenella creeping away by herself, and she was really upset when she saw how sad the little girl looked. She ran to her.

"Don't you look like that, my lovey! It's that sharp-tongued aunt of yours, I suppose. Why didn't you tell me it was your own kind little heart and clever fingers that made that suit for Jimmy? Silly child! If you'd told me that I'm not have said a word."

"Everyone's so angry with me," sobbed Fenella. "Even Willie!"

"You come into my caravan and talk to me," said Mrs. Connie. "Things go wrong sometimes, but they soon clear up if we face them properly. You come along with me."

The little monkey woman had the kindest heart in the world. She made a fuss of Fenny. She gave her a big slice of gingerbread with peel in it, and put a glass of sweet lemonade before her.

"To think you made that beautiful little suit!" she said. "Well, well! You're a marvel. It fits Jimmy like a glove. It was like you, Fenny, to think of a thing like that and never say a word. Your aunt will get over it, never you fear. As for Willie, he'll get over his sulks, too. He's a nice boy, but he's too big for his boots sometimes. A hiding won't hurt him."

"But he thinks it's all because of *me*," said Fenella. She took a bite of the cake. It was delicious. She sipped the lemonade and began to feel better. It was nice to have someone fussing her like this.

She began to tell Mrs. Connie everything. The little monkey woman listened patiently. Grin came to the door of the caravan and she waved him away. He always turned up when cake was about. Fenny didn't even see him. She went on talking, and felt better and better as she poured out everything to Mrs. Connie.

She told her about the money and how she wanted to

buy a sewing-machine for Aunt Lou, and how her aunt had vowed she wouldn't let her have it. She told her about Mr. Presto and how he had said she was ungrateful, and had been so cross too.

"What shall I do?" she asked. "How can I make Willie believe me? And do you think Aunt Aggie will be cross as well, and not help me with stuff to make Bobbo a little clown suit? I did want to start this evening."

"Oh, Aggie will be all right," said Mrs. Connie, making up her mind to run across and tell her how unhappy Fenella was, and that she really hadn't meant to get Willie into trouble. "Don't you worry about that. If I were you I'd keep away from Lou till she's got her temper back again. She'll be all right soon. You go across to Aggie's and sew there. And if Willie's there, just talk to him as if nothing had happened. He can't keep it up for long."

"All right," said Fenella, feeling more cheerful. "And I'll go to-morrow and see if I can buy that sewing-machine for Aunt Lou."

Mrs. Connie looked in amazement at Fenella. "What! You'd do that even after she's scolded you like this! You're a forgiving child, Fenny. I wish you were mine!"

"It might make Aunt Lou feel happier if she knew I wanted to give her something," said Fenella. "I don't *feel* as if I want to, really, at this very moment, Mrs. Connie—I feel that she's horrid and mean. But I know that things would be so much easier if she had a sewing-machine—she wouldn't need to work so hard, and she'd love it."

Aunt Lou didn't bother about where Fenella was. She was so annoyed with her for making the little suit for Jimmy, and not saying anything about it. Uncle Ursie did not make things any better when he stuck up for Fenny.

"She only did it out of the kindness of her heart, so that you wouldn't have to, and so that Mr. Crack wouldn't turn us all out for your defiance," he said. "I wonder you can't see that, Lou. Would you have said the same if our little Carol had done it? No—you'd have thought she was a clever, kind little kid, you know you would. You've changed, Lou. Carol wouldn't know you for her mother if she was alive now."

Aunt Lou was horrified to hear such a thing from kindly old Ursie. She took a quick look at herself in the glass. She saw her grim face, the hard, thin-lipped mouth and the cross-looking eyes. No, Carol wouldn't know her now!

"Fenny's so like Carol," said Ursie. "She's like her in looks, with that mane of red hair, and she's like her in ways. Look at the way she gets on with the animals, and yet she was never in a circus before. Mark my words, Lou, you won't keep that child long if you treat her harshly. She'll be writing to her aunt in Canada to take her away, and I don't blame her. But I should miss her now."

Aunt Lou began to feel most uncomfortable. There was a lot of truth in Ursie's words. Then her temper rose again and she spoke spitefully to him.

"You're a soft old man, that's what you are! And Fenny's not so simple and sweet as you think she is!"

Uncle Ursie went out, cross and unhappy. People like Lou made so much trouble in the world! What a pity.

Fenella stayed with Mrs. Connie till tea-time, for she really did not dare to go and see if her aunt wanted her to help with any sewing. After that she went across to Aunt Aggie's caravan. Mrs. Connie had already been to see her and had explained things. Aunt Aggie, knowing Willie's way of sulking at times, nodded her head.

"Don't you worry, Connie. I'll make Fenny welcome. I'm sure the child didn't really tell tales of Willie. She's not that sort. You send her here. If Willie's in the sulks, he can stay out."

So Fenella came timidly to Aunt Aggie's caravan and was made very welcome. "I'm going to be hard at work," announced Fenella. "That is, if you'll give me some

147

more stuff to sew, Aunt Aggie. I want to make something for Mr. Presto, to show him that really and truly I *am* grateful for all he has taught me. And I'm going to make a new bonnet for Cackles to show Willie I'm sorry for making him unhappy. And I'd like to start the little clown suit for Bobbo."

Willie was not there. He came in once, saw Fenella, and went out again, scowling. Nobody took any notice of him. Fenella found some gold stars in one of Aunt Aggie's boxes and was thrilled. "May I have these? I want to make a little black mat for Cinders to sit on, when Mr. Presto draws a chalk circle round her to do some magic. And if I sew some stars on, it will match Mr. Presto's cloak and caravan!"

The little mat was soon finished. It looked very grand with its pattern of gold stars. Aunt Aggie admired it very much.

"You're clever, Fenny! And it took you no time at all to make it! Whatever will you do next!"

"I'm turning this old straw hat of Rosebud's into a bonnet for Cackles," said Fenella, pleased at Aunt Aggie's admiration. "That won't take me long either. It's going to have little red ribbons hanging down the back. Cackles will look sweet in it!"

It was tried on Cackles an hour later when it was finished. Cackles certainly looked beautiful, and rather fancied herself. She waddled across the floor of the caravan showing off her new bonnet.

"Look, Willie!" said Aunt Aggie, as Willie appeared suddenly. "What do you think of Cackles' new bonnet?"

Willie gave it a glance. He thought it was very fine indeed. But he wasn't going to say so! "It's all right," he said ungraciously, and disappeared again.

Then Fenella had an hour left to start Bobbo's clown suit. Aunt Aggie had given her some fine white stuff that had once been a cloak. It was just the thing. Fenella began to cut out the suit, frowning, as she tried to think out exactly how it should go.

She was sorry when she had to stop. "Well, you ought

to feel better now," said Aunt Aggie, and gave her an unexpected good-night kiss. "You've been doing things for other people all the evening. There's nothing like that for making things come right!"

HAS FENELLA RUN AWAY

THE next day Fenella remembered that she meant to go and buy her aunt a sewing-machine. Aunt Lou had been a little nicer to her, but not much. Uncle Ursie had been exactly the same as usual. Willie still avoided her, and would not say a word.

She went to her lessons at ten o'clock. Willie was there before her! He wasn't going to risk being tackled by Mr. Crack again.

"Ah, nice and early this morning, I am pleased to see!" said Presto. Fenella gave him a little parcel.

"You're always giving *me* presents. So now I've made *you* one," she said. "At least, it's for Cinders. I just wanted you to know I *am* grateful for all the time you spend on me."

Presto opened the parcel. When he saw the beautiful little mat, embroidered with its gold stars, he was touched and pleased. "Now that is very kind of you, Fenella," he said. "You do not sulk or bear malice when people scold you. I am proud of you. Here, Cinders, sit on this and be proud to have such a fine mat of your own. We will take it into the ring with us when next we go!"

Willie did not look pleased. "Sucking up again," he muttered under his breath.

"I'm not," said Fenella indignantly. "Didn't I make Cackles a new bonnet last night? Well, I wasn't sucking up to *you*, was I? I just wanted to show you I was sorry you'd been in a row."

Willie said no more. He had really been very pleased

with the little bonnet, but he always found it difficult to come out of his sulks once he had got them badly.

Aunt Lou and Uncle Ursie were going to be busy that afternoon. "I've got to go and see to all Mr. Crack's clothes in his caravan, and look them over," she said to Ursie. "I'll be back for tea, though."

"I'm going to take Clump and Bobbo down to the shore," said Uncle Ursie. "It's so hot. What are *you* doing, Fenny? Coming with me?"

"Well, no, if you don't mind," said Fenella. "I've got some thing important to do."

"All right," said Uncle Ursie, thinking perhaps she was going off with Willie and the dogs. "See you at tea-time."

"Yes, I'll be here," said Fenella. "I'll put the kettle on to boil ready for you."

Aunt Lou took her work-basket and went. Uncle Ursie fetched the bears and disappeared down the cliff path. As soon as they had gone Fenny went to her doll's trunk. Where was that five pounds?

It wasn't there! It was gone! Fenella kept on feeling through all the clothes, but no, the money was not there. She guessed then that Aunt Lou must have taken it. She stood in the caravan, her face red, tears starting in her eyes. Then she blinked them back. It was silly to keep wanting to cry when things went wrong. Willie hadn't cried even when he had been whipped by Mr. Crack the day before.

She thought hard. "Aunt Lou didn't know what I wanted the money for, else she surely would have let me use it. Well, I'll go and ask Mrs. Connie to lend me some, and I'll pay her back when I get Uncle Ursie to give me more money. Oh, dear— I do wish Aunt Lou had *told* me she was going to take it away. But I suppose she did it because *I* didn't tell her about making that suit for Jimmy."

She went to Mrs. Connie's caravan and told her she needed the money. "Uncle Ursie has gone down to the shore, or I'd ask him," she said. "Could *you* lend me
150

some, please, Mrs. Connie? You know that I'll pay you back this evening when I get it from Uncle Ursie."

Most circus folk are generous and eager to help one another. Mrs. Connie didn't hesitate for a moment. Fenny wanted the money—and she wanted it for a kindly deed, too. Then she should have it! Lou had taken that money out of the doll's trunk, had she? Then she, Mrs. Connie, would be all the more pleased to let Fenny have the same amount! She counted out four pounds in pound and ten shilling notes, and a pound in silver coins.

"There you are," she said. "You take the bus at the gate, and you get out at the ninth stop. That's the town of Merring-on-Sea. There's some fine big shops there. You'll have to ask them to *send* the machine, you know. It will be too heavy to carry. I only hope it won't cost more than five pounds!"

Fenella set off. She saw Willie in the distance and waved to him. But he didn't wave back, and she felt sad. She caught the bus and was soon trundling away through the country-side.

Tea-time came. Aunt Lou came across from Mr. Crack's caravan after a hard afternoon's work. She frowned when she saw there was no kettle boiling. She had been hoping that Fenella would have had the kettle ready and bread and butter cut. If she had, Aunt Lou was quite prepared to be better-tempered!

Uncle Ursie came up from the shore with two wet and happy bears. They had all had a lovely time. Uncle Ursie was never so happy as when he was with his bears. He had been with bears and seals all his life, and to him they were like his children.

"Where's Fenny?" he said. "I suppose she's not back yet. I was hoping to tell her all about Bobbo's antics this afternoon. He's a real comic."

Fenella didn't come after tea. She hadn't arrived by six o'clock. Uncle Ursie went across to Willie. "Have you seen Fenny?" he asked.

"Not since she caught the bus at two o'clock this

151

afternoon," said Willie. "Why, isn't she back? Where did she go?"

It was news to Uncle Ursie that Fenella had gone off by bus. He was puzzled. He went to Aunt Lou and told her.

"Where can the child have gone?" he said. "I hope she'll come back soon."

But seven o'clock came and no Fenella. Uncle Ursie couldn't sit still. "You don't think she's run off, do you, Lou?" he said. "She's been very unhappy, you know. It would be dreadful if we lost Fenny, as well as Carol."

Aunt Lou began to be alarmed, too. She wished she hadn't scolded Fenny so hard. After all, the child hadn't done any harm—she had only tried to put things right without telling her. She went across to Mrs. Connie.

"Have you seen Fenella?" she asked gruffly, for she hadn't spoken to Mrs. Connie since she had quarrelled with her the day before.

Mrs. Connie saw that Lou was anxious and she was pleased. She wasn't going to tell her where Fenny had gone, or why! No, let her think the child had run away! That would do Lou good to think she had driven a child away by her harshness!

"Fenny came and borrowed five pounds from me," said Mrs. Connie. "Then off she went."

"Good gracious! Five pounds!" said Aunt Lou, remembering guiltily the money she had removed from the doll's trunk. "Oh, Connie—has the child run away? Has she taken the five pounds to try and get out to Canada! Maybe a child would think it wouldn't cost more than that."

"Lou, if Fenny ran away I wouldn't blame her," said Mrs. Connie. "You had one dear little girl, and you lost her—and here you have another sent to you, and you treat her unkindly, and she runs away. What's the matter with you? You need a change of heart. Ursie will run away from you one day, too!"

Aunt Lou turned away miserably. She felt quite sure now that Fenny had run away. The police would find her, no doubt—and everyone would know Fenny had run away because she, her Aunt Lou, had treated her badly. She had shut her heart to Fenny. Fenny wasn't Carol, but she was like her, and Aunt Lou wouldn't have anyone in her heart but Carol. She was wrong, very wrong. She had lost her chance of having another child growing up and loving her.

When nine o'clock came everyone in the camp was alarmed. They all knew now that Fenny had gone by the two o'clock bus and hadn't come back. Mrs. Connie also began to think, as everyone else did, that Fenny had run away. "She just made the buying of that sewing-machine an excuse," she said to herself. "She'd have been back long ago if she'd just gone for that. Poor Ursie, he does look bad. He was fond of that little niece of his."

Presto wanted to take Mr. Crack's car and go off and look for Fenny. Mr. Crack wanted to telephone the police. But the circus folk always kept away from the police if they could, so nobody thought much of that idea.

Aunt Aggie was crying. "I wanted her to come and sew with me this evening," she said. "I waited for her. She was making a clown suit for Bobbo."

"She brought me a lovely little mat for Cinders," said Presto. "She was a kind child. Mr. Crack, we must do *something* to find her!"

Mr. Holla and Mr. Tiny said they would go out and look for her. Everyone wanted to do something. Willie was simply horrified to think that Fenny really might have run away.

He went to his mother. "Mum, I didn't even wave to Fenny when she went to catch the bus. And I haven't spoken to her all day If I'd been decent she wouldn't have gone, I'm sure. If only she'll come back safe and sound I'll make it up to her."

Aggie wiped her tears. "Yes, you've done your share in making her unhappy," she said. "But, mark my words, she won't come back."

This made Willie feel more wretched than ever. He was thoroughly ashamed of himself now, and wanted to make things up to Fenny and see her smile at him. Cackles knew he was unhappy and pressed herself against him.

Uncle Ursie went to Aunt Lou in the caravan. She was sitting at the table doing nothing. Uncle Ursie spoke to her.

"Lou! If Fenny has really run away, and is found and brought back, ought we to make her stay if she doesn't want to? You don't want the child, do you? If you'd rather she didn't come back to us again, I can arrange it. I'm fond of the child myself, but if you don't want her, and she doesn't want to live with us, I'll see she goes somewhere else where maybe she'll be happy."

To Uncle Ursie's immense amazement Aunt Lou burst into tears, a thing he had not seen her do for years. "I do want her!" sobbed Aunt Lou. "I wouldn't take to her because she wasn't Carol. But now I'll love her because she's Fenny. Suppose something's happened to her, Ursie! I'll blame myself all my life long, just like I blamed myself for Carol. If only she comes back safe and sound I'll soon show her I want her. I've been cruel and hard—but if Fenny comes back I'll be different."

"Poor Lou," said Uncle Ursie, and put his arms round her. "Don't take on so. You just show the child we want her, when she comes back. Then she'll be as right as rain."

"But where *is* she?" said Aunt Lou anxiously. And that is what all the circus folk were saying. "Where *is* Fenny?"

BRAVO, FENNY !

JUST as Mr. Crack was getting into his car to go out
and search for Fenny with Presto, a shout went up
from someone at the gate.

"Here she is!"

And sure enough, there she was—a very tired, limping
little Fenny, scared of the dark, and very much afraid
of being scolded by everyone. Mr. Crack ran to her and
swept her off her feet.

"Here she is, bless her! Where have you been, you
scamp? You've given us a real scare!"

"Fenny! I'm so glad you've come back!" That was
Willie. He tried to hug her, but could only reach her
legs, as she was on Mr. Crack's shoulder. "Oh, Fenny,
I've been so worried about you."

Then Uncle Ursie and Aunt Lou came running up,
too. "Give her to me," commanded Aunt Lou, and Mr.
Crack put her down. To Fenny's great surprise and
pleasure Aunt Lou put her arms round her and hugged
her. She pressed her cheek against Fenny's and wouldn't
let her go.

"You shouldn't run away," she kept saying. "You
shouldn't. You shouldn't. But, thanks be, you've come
back!"

Uncle Ursie hugged her, too. Fenny felt more and
more surprised and pleased. She had been expecting
plenty of scoldings, not all this petting and kindness.
Everyone crowded round, trying to get in a word or a
pat.

"I couldn't do without my good little pupil!" said
Presto's deep voice, and Fenny looked up at him and
smiled. He smiled back, a sudden and delightful smile
that made his whole face look different.

"Mr. Presto! You've smiled!" cried Fenella. "You
did, you did. And you vowed you never would. Please
smile again."

Aunt Aggie, Mrs. Connie, Wriggle and all the others

155

came to make sure that Fenny was really back again. It was most astonishing to see how the little girl had made her way into their hearts during the short time she had been with them. Aunt Lou couldn't help feeling proud to see what affection they had for her.

She was carried back to the red caravan by Ursie. Mr. Crack came with them. He wanted to find out what had happened to Fenella.

"I didn't run away," said Fenella, surprised that anyone should think she had. "Why should I? I like being with the circus. I just went to buy Aunt Lou a sewing-machine with some money I got yesterday."

There was a dead silence. Aunt Lou swallowed a lump that had suddenly come into her throat. Fenny went on. "I borrowed some money from Mrs. Connie and I went. There wasn't a sewing-machine shop in the first town, so I went on to the next and found one there."

"And did they sell you a sewing-machine?" said Mr. Crack, very much interested in Fenny's story.

"No, they wouldn't, because I hadn't enough money and because they said I was only a child," said Fenella. "I was awfully disappointed. But they gave me this paper, look, Aunt Lou. And if you'll fill it in and send it to them, with the money, they will send you a lovely machine. I saw it. I shall love using it, too! "

Aunt Lou couldn't say a word.

"You're too good to be true, Fenny," said Uncle Ursie. "Here's your Aunt Lou been scolding you for all she was worth—and all you do is to go out and buy her a sewing-machine. I never knew such a kid. Lou, the next three times she's naughty, we won't scold her at all, will we?"

"No," said Aunt Lou, her face looking younger and softer than it had for years.

"Won't you really?" said Fenny in delight. "Oh, then I'll do some things I've longed to do. I'll take Bobbo to bed with me one night and let him sleep there all night through! "

Everyone laughed. "Well, what happened next?" asked Mr. Crack.

"I went down to the seashore at that town," said Fenny, "and I stayed too late to catch the bus back here. I didn't know it went so early. So I had to walk all the way back. That's all. I thought you'd be very cross with me for being late."

"All's well that end's well," said Mr. Crack, opening the door of the caravan. "Go to sleep now, Fenella, for you must be tired out."

Fenella was soon in bed. Aunt Lou bent down and kissed her. Fenella was so surprised that she didn't kiss her back. Then she put her arms round Aunt Lou's neck.

"You're nice," she said sleepily. "Always be nice, Aunt Lou. I love you when you're nice."

Fenella soon forgot about her adventure, but the circus folk didn't. Willie didn't let Fenny out of his sight after that. Mr. Presto, once he had remembered how to produce a smile, found that he had plenty, and it was nice to use them.

"Why didn't you smile before?" asked Fenella one morning. "I do want to know."

"It's something I want to forget," said Presto, "and if I tell you I shan't forget it, shall I? I shall forget it soon, if you keep making me smile. Now what about a spot of magic this morning? Shall we have Cinders in, and see what happens?"

It was Aunt Lou that made things so much nicer for Fenny. She still had a sharp tongue if things didn't go right, but she showed Fenny that she was fond of her, and she accepted the sewing-machine with so much pleasure that Fenny laughed to see her aunt's delight.

"I never saw such a clever machine!" she said. "Never! Do you mean to tell me it does all those different stitches? Well, I never did! Let's use it this very afternoon."

"We can go on with the clown suit I'm making for Bobbo," said Fenella. "We could finish it between us.

Can we, Aunt Lou? Then we'll try it on him. He'll look so sweet."

He did! The little white clown suit with its black bobbles fitted him well, and the clown hat that went with it gave him a most comical look. He capered about clumsily and everyone clapped him. He sat down suddenly and looked round in surprise. Then he clapped his paws together solemnly.

"Can we go into the ring one night?" begged Fenella of Uncle Ursie. "Willie and I have been practising with Bobbo every day now. The circus opens again tomorrow. Can't I just *try*, Uncle Ursie!"

"Mr. Crack has to decide that," said Uncle Ursie. "You ask him to see your turn with Willie, Cackles and Bobbo, and hear what he says. I think it's very good myself. Maybe he'll let you try."

"And can I have a very, very pretty frock?" asked Fenella. "We could make one, couldn't we, Aunt Lou?"

"Yes. I could make you a lovely one," said Aunt Lou. "I've got some frilly stuff for a skirt. And you could have a little cloak edged with red like Willie's if you like."

"Oh, I'd like wings edged with red instead!" said Fenny. "I've always wanted to have a fairy's dress. Uncle Ursie, *please* ask Mr. Crack if he'll see our turn."

Mr. Crack said he would. He turned up in the ring that afternoon. Willie, Fenny, Bobbo, Cackles and Uncle Ursie were there waiting for him. Aunt Lou was watching from the seats. Mr. Crack joined her and nodded his head for Willie to come in with Cackles.

He watched with great interest and a good deal of astonishment from beginning to end of the carefully rehearsed turn. Willie was as good as ever with his bird imitations, and with Cackles—but this time there was Bobbo as well, in his little clown suit, waddling here and there, balancing himself on his big ball, going after balloons, following Cackles into her house and banging at the door!

And there was Fenny, too, guiding him and helping
158

him, rather nervous, but determined to show Bobbo off to the very best advantage.

"Very good indeed," said Mr. Crack at last, and Aunt Lou began to clap. "Willie, I have a mind to let you and Fenny try this turn together. If it goes flat, Fenny can step out. If it's a success, she can stay in. Bobbo is very good—a natural little bear-clown. You get them sometimes like that. Fenny is a marvel with him. A very good little show."

Fenny almost ran to him and hugged him. But he was the great Mr. Crack, and she was still rather scared of him, so she didn't. She just stood and beamed. Willie squeezed her arm.

"We'll bring the house down!" he whispered. "Now you'll have to get busy with that new dress of yours, Fenny."

Soon the camp was busy once more with its preparations for the next shown. Its short holiday was over. Now to work again!

The circus folk were glad. They liked the excitement of dressing up, the glare of the lights in the big top at night, the shouts and cries, the cheers and clapping. It was their life and they could not be happy for long without it.

And now Fenella, too, felt the same excitement. Her fingers trembled as she put on the beautiful little fairy dress Aunt Lou had made for her. Uncle Ursie dressed Bobbo, who was just as excited as Fenny herself. He tried to turn head-over-heels with his hat on.

"*Not* with your hat on, Bobbo," said Uncle Ursie. "Take it off first. How many more times am I to tell you that?"

The great evening had come. Hundreds of people streamed in at the gate, eager to see the wonderful show. Drums sounded and trumpets blew to welcome them. The ring was strewn with clean, fresh sawdust. Everything was ready—and the show began.

Shall we peep in? Here we are in the middle of the show. What is going on? A boy stands in the centre of the ring, whistling and fluting like a dozen birds. Then he quacks like a duck—he cries like a seagull—and the seagulls outside answer him and swoop down to the tent.

And now here is a little girl coming in. How pretty she looks with her red hair fluffed round her excited face. Her frilly skirt bounces up and down and she has white wings edged with bright red.

"She's a fairy!" whisper all the watching children around. "She's a fairy. And, oh, look—is that a tiny clown?"

Yes, it is. It's Bobbo, of course, proud to wear his beautiful clown suit, eager to get claps and cheers from all these watching people. How comical he is! And look at that goose coming out of the little house to do her shopping!

Everyone roars with laughter. Cackles does her shopping—and Bobbo follows behind, trying to get her basket from her.

"Look out, Cackles, he nearly had it! Aha, serve him right, you pecked him very neatly. But he doesn't care! He's off after that big ball."

So the four of them give their first turn, and when at last Cackles goes to her house and slams the door, and Bobbo follows and knocks loudly, there is such a howl of laughter that even Mr. Crack, peering with delight through the red curtains, is surprised.

"Bravo, Fenny! Bravo, Bobbo!" he shouts as they come out together, Bobbo's paw in Fenny's hand. "Well done, Willie, well done, Cackles! A very fine performance."

And we must clap, too, and shout loudly. Bravo, Fenny! Bravo! You deserve your success, and so does little Bobbo. You're just at the beginning of things now. What will you do in the future?

Well, that's another story. I must tell it to you some day!